RUTTING SEASON

SEASON

– Stories –

MANDELIENE SMITH

SCRIBNER

New York London Toronto Sydney New Delhi

Scribner

An Imprint of Simon & Schuster, Inc.

1230 Avenue of the Americas

New York, NY 10020

First Scribner hardcover edition February 2019

SCRIBNER and design are registered trademarks of The Gale Group, Inc., used under license by Simon & Schuster, Inc., the publisher of this work.

For information about special discounts for bulk purchases, please contact Simon & Schuster Special Sales at 1-866-506-1949 or business@simonandschuster.com.

The Simon & Schuster Speakers Bureau can bring authors to your live event. For more information or to book an event contact the Simon & Schuster Speakers Bureau at 1-866-248-3049 or visit our website at www.simonspeakers.com.

Interior design by Kyle Kabel

Manufactured in the United States of America

1   3   5   7   9   10   8   6   4   2

Library of Congress Cataloging-in-Publication data is available.

ISBN 978-1-5011-9270-8
ISBN 978-1-5011-9272-2 (ebook)

Some of the stories in this volume were previously published, including "Friday Night," which first appeared in *New England Review*; "Mercy" in *The Sun*; "Rutting Season" in *Guernica*; and "Animals" in *The Massachusetts Review*.

For my parents

CONTENTS

RUTTING
SEASON

MERCY

The children's puppy was run over at the end of May. Not on the main road, which Pam might have expected, but on the dirt track that formed the western boundary of the farm. How was it possible? No one even drove there. But there he was, splayed out in the lush, green weeds of the shoulder, his sweet muzzle soaked with blood. Pam wrapped him in her coat and carried him across the field to the house, his body still soft in her arms.

With the kittens, the vet thought it was some sort of congenital defect. The goldfish were most likely from over-feeding—no surprise there, given the twins' fascination with the food shaker. And the duckling? Who knew? Pam didn't need to settle on a definite culprit, but the children did. The children needed an explanation for everything.

"What animal ate Duckle?" Jack asked again. This time he wasn't looking at her; he was pounding his hot dog head-first in a puddle of ketchup.

Pam turned back to the sink, unconsciously shutting out the sight of his smooth, too-serious face. He was seven years old and his father was dead. The list of things she couldn't protect him from had suddenly become infinite.

"I don't know, sweetheart," she said lightly. "Maybe a fox?"

"Or a raccoon?"

"Or a raccoon."

"Which?"

She could not escape. The chicks died, the barn cat came down with distemper, the goats wandered out onto the rotten ice of the pond and drowned. By the time Aidan's hamster disappeared she was beyond caring; she was in a whirl of fury, like a horse maddened by flies. Besides, she had always hated the hamster.

"How could you hate a hamster?" asked her best friend, Trish.

"Oh, I don't know." Pam held the phone with her shoulder as she scooped the warm clothes out of the dryer. She saw again the little curved teeth, the furry face. "It was just greedy, you know? Greedy and self-serving."

"It was a hamster! What'd you expect, Gandhi?"

"No, really, I'm telling you, all that thing cared about was eating. It would have eaten its own ass if it could have gotten its mouth around it."

Trish laughed and Pam felt the heaviness inside her ease up a little. To laugh, to make a joke, however feeble, restored to her a sense of herself as someone normal—a mother, a woman in the world. She stuffed another load into the machine and let the lid slam shut.

"What's that noise? You're not doing more laundry, are you? Seriously," Trish added in a gentler tone, "it's late. You should go to bed."

Pam sighed. "I wish. I've still got the barn to do."

"Okay, pioneer woman."

It was their old, half-serious dispute. Why take on so much? Why make life so complicated? Trish kept things simple: one child, one cat; a backyard just big enough for a swing set and a patio.

"Don't worry," Pam said. "At the rate we're going, every living thing on this place will be dead by July and I'll just sit around eating bonbons."

There was a heavy pause. "Joke," Pam said, but it was too late.

"Are you really okay?"

"Yeah, I'm okay," Pam said. She pictured Trish putting the phone down and padding down the hall to relay their conversation to her husband, Brian. A bitter envy rose in her.

"You call," Trish said. "One a.m., whatever."

"I know," Pam said, "thanks." After they hung up, she lay down on the kitchen floor to wait. The grief came in a surge: savage, shocking. She cried hard for a few minutes; then she wiped her eyes, got up, and went back to folding clothes.

—

Brian had died six months earlier of a massive coronary. There was nothing Pam could have done even if she had been there, and she hadn't; she'd been inside cooking dinner. When he didn't come in on time, she had stomped out to the barn, fired up with her habitual annoyance (he dallied over everything), and found him lying facedown in the frozen mud of the paddock. He had been thawing the horses' water. They weren't even his concern, the horses. He was a lawyer, not a farmer; he didn't even like to ride. Yet he would do such a thing—to help her out, to revel in the crazy, animal-filled circus that was his home life. He had loved all of that: the chickens sneaking into the sunroom, the mice making nests in the horse blankets, the rich, crowing absurdity of having three children and six horses and four dogs and two cats and God only knew how many chickens and goats and ducks. He would come home from work and stretch out on the couch, sated, an only child surrounded by fecundity.

It was up to Pam to say no, to set limits, to buy life insurance and save for the kids' college. She was vigilant, always. Her father had died young, and she knew how quickly things could go bad. But Brian had believed—if not in God then in his own good fortune: Pam was the best; the kids were the best; everything would be fine. But he had been wrong.

She was bitter, she knew it; her heart was clenched like a fist. The last time Reverend Pratt had come by, she'd barely been civil. She was cleaning the bridles in the tack room when she saw his car coming up the driveway. For a second she had thought about pretending she didn't hear him or slipping out the back, but she stayed where she was; she answered his call and waited while he followed her voice to the tack room. The proper thing would have been to take him up to the house and make him some coffee but she didn't; she offered him a hay bale to sit on and went on with her work.

"Thank you, Pamela," he said, lowering himself gingerly onto the prickly surface.

She and the kids hadn't been to church since the funeral. That was what he'd talked about on his previous visit: He thought the children needed the continuity. But this time he didn't mention church. Instead he talked of "God's mercy."

"God's plan is something we just can't know," he said in his wavering, old man's voice. He went on: He knew how hard it was; God knew how it hard it was. Hadn't He given His only son? "We just have to trust in His mercy," he said.

Pam scraped her fingernail along the bridle's dirty stitching and turned her hand over to study the brownish green gunk that had balled up under her nail. He wanted to talk about God? Fine, let him talk. When he was done, she let him peck her cheek and then watched him walk to his car with a piece of hay dangling from his pants.

Reverend Pratt came to defend God, she told Brian. *He sat on a hay bale.*

That was it? Brian said. *Reverend Pratt on a hay bale? No thunder? No whirlwind?*

Pam laughed. But the truth was she didn't know what Brian would have said, and she never would. Staring at the empty square of gravel where Reverend Pratt's car had been, she suddenly knew she couldn't make it through another minute.

But she did, of course. She made it and made it and made it.

—

Pam finished folding the laundry and put the basket at the base of the stairs so she would remember to bring it up. She glanced at the clock as she pulled on her boots. Trish was right, it was late, but Pam liked the evening barn work. The solitude and quiet were soothing after the hectic pace of the day. She shoved the plastic baby monitor in her back pocket and went out into the fragrant June dark. She breathed in the exhalation of the cooling earth. The crying had released her a little, and now the sensations of the world flooded back: the scent of the linden tree, the damp air lifting the tiny hairs on her arms. She let herself stop inside the barn door to listen to the horses eating hay in their steady, peaceful way. It was the sound of comfort and routine, of everything as it should be.

The farm had been Brian's idea. If he had to be married to a horse person, why not move out to where the horses were? That way he'd at least get to catch a glimpse of her galloping by. It was the kind of quip he used at cocktail parties and barbecues, places where he was likely to meet other beleaguered horse husbands, but the truth was he had been generous about her need to ride, even after the twins were born. "Go, crazy lady," he'd say, shaking his head in amusement, and she would put on her riding boots and go, her body light with relief.

What was it she loved so much? Riding was hard, hot work, repetitive and often frustrating, and yet she always felt better afterward. It untangled her, somehow, to engage in that physical call and response, to guide, through the live wires of the reins, the pressure of her legs, that spectacularly powerful body, that wild, mostly unknowable mind.

They were down to only six now: three boarders, two ponies for the kids, and Ace, Pam's four-year-old Thoroughbred. Ace was the best she'd ever had, the first with a chance of competing at the advanced level, but when Brian died, training him had become just another low priority, like getting a haircut or cleaning the car. She went to his stall and he stretched his head over the door to sniff her face with his soft, whiskery nostrils. He was a beauty, a real mover. Even when he was hacking around in the pasture you could see it—the springing stride, that natural ease. And he had heart, meaning that he was willing, that he would give you everything he had, not because you forced him, but because that was how he was.

People had begun to suggest that she sell him. Her mother-in-law, her sister; even Trish had tried to bring it up. They thought it was too much, caring for all those horses—too much time, too much money, too risky leaving the kids alone every morning. Those were all reasons Pam could dismiss, but there was another, better one: She had no right to keep him if she was going to let him go to waste. She ran her hand along the crest of his neck. Already he had lost muscle.

I should sell him, she told herself, and a rush of anger went through her. *Trish,* she thought, suddenly remembering something that had happened the week before, *goddamn Trish.*

It was at a birthday party for one of Alice and Aidan's friends, a real production, with a dozen three-year-olds, a trampoline, an ice cream cake. Pam and Trish and Lacey, another mom, had stayed to help. Or that was the idea, anyway. In fact, Trish and Lacey had disappeared halfway through. Pam hadn't even noticed; she was rushing around in her usual way, anticipating dangers, fielding demands. When she came upon them talking in the kitchen, she stopped in surprise.

"Every night?" Lacey was saying.

"I kid you not," Trish said. "We have to order condoms in these boxes, I mean like this." She showed the size of the box with her hands.

"Oh my God!"

They both laughed. Then Trish looked up and saw her, and the amusement died away in her eyes.

Now, in the quiet of the barn, Pam saw again their turning faces, bright with laughter and sweat, and herself in the doorway behind them—sexless, drab, a figure who stood aside.

I kid you not.

She leaned over the stall door and pressed her hot face against Ace's neck. Her brain lurched in the sudden dark. She was tired, she was much more tired than she'd realized. Through the thick plane of his muscle, she could feel the grinding of his teeth, the quick jerk of his head as he tugged more hay from the net. Slowly her face cooled, her mind went quiet.

In the months since Brian had died, she had lost all taste for the wants of her body. She ate but she had no appetite, and afterward she often felt nauseated, as though she had forced herself to do something unnatural. Washing was worse and most days she didn't bother, so her short, blond hair was frequently dark with grease. Dimly, she knew this; she knew that people noticed, but she could not bring herself to shower more often. Her breasts, her belly, her thighs, even the sensation of hot water on her scalp—all this had belonged in some part to Brian, or to their pairing. To see her own flushed skin, to run the soap over the muscles of her arms and legs, felt like a betrayal. That part of the life of her body was over; she wanted it to be over. And yet when she had come upon Trish and Lacey laughing, she had felt the stab of exclusion.

She opened her eyes and looked at the line of shovels and forks hanging along the barn wall. The neat row of handles spoke of order and calm: the tools in their places, the children safe. Why not start riding again? What harm could it do? An hour or so while the kids were in school.

She straightened up, buoyed; her exhaustion had drained away. She swung open the stall door and let Ace bomb down the aisle to the paddock. Then she put the baby monitor on the windowsill and started mucking his stall.

—

"Guess what we've got for breakfast?" Pam said. "Bagels! Alice, get away from that fish tank."

Alice's face took on a stony aspect, as though she'd suddenly gone deaf. She reached over the back of the chair she was standing on and touched the dirty surface of the water with one small finger.

Pam suppressed a flash of irritation. "I've got cinnamon raisin!" she said in the singsong, kindergarten voice she despised. Alice spun around.

Bribery and manipulation, manipulation and bribery—really, she was getting worse and worse. But today she didn't care. She had woken early, not with her usual dread, but with a sense of expectation. She had thought through the logistics as she lay among her sleeping children. (None of them spent a full night on their own anymore; she couldn't bring herself to make them.) If she put off going to the feed store, if she skipped lunch, if she left Ace in the paddock instead of turning him loose with the others—she could squeeze in an hour, anyway. It was a start.

She put half a bagel on each plate, and a spoonful of cream

cheese; then a handful of Cheerios, then banana slices. Food and backup food. She needed ten minutes, fifteen at the outside to get the morning barn work done. She had it down like a drill: run up the driveway, dump the grain, toss the chicken feed, put the halters on the horses, let them out, shut the doors so they wouldn't get into the grain bins (even an hour of gorging on grain could kill a horse). Still, ten minutes was a long time; ten minutes was a minefield, and today she'd need a little extra time to get Ace set up in the paddock. She walked over and latched the door that led to the stairs.

"Raisin!" Alice said to Aidan, holding up her bagel.

Pam grabbed one of her boots from behind the door and pulled it on.

"Mama," Aidan said in his slow, deliberate voice.

"Yes?" She pulled on the other boot.

He lifted his eyes to her solemnly. "Can I det a durtle?"

She stopped, pierced.

"He said 'turtle,'" Alice said.

"I know, sweetie, thanks." Pam bent down and kissed Aidan's head. "Sure, we can get you a turtle." *It might live*, she thought. And she wouldn't have to get him another hamster. She put an extra blob of cream cheese on each of their plates to boost the entertainment value and grabbed the baby monitor. The dogs crowded up against the door, jumping and whining.

"Jack, you're in charge," she said, pushing the dogs back with her leg.

"I know," he said.

She opened the door and the dogs shot out. It was a beautiful clear day; her heart lifted. Outside the barn, she scooped up the dead bluebird by the fence and tossed it onto the manure pile without a thought.

She was already letting the horses into the pasture when she heard something over the monitor. She rolled the wooden door shut and stopped to listen: nothing, overamplified silence. Ace whinnied frantically in his stall. Pam went back to him and slipped the halter over his bobbing head. Then she led him down the aisle to the door that opened onto the paddock.

"I'm gonna tell Mom." That was Jack.

The next sound came through in a burst of static. A crash? An explosion? Pam let go of Ace's halter and whirled around. She heard him clatter out the door as she ran the opposite way, toward the house.

She found them standing on the chairs, unhurt, above a flood of greenish water. She swallowed a wild urge to laugh: It was only the fish tank, and it wasn't even broken.

"It fell!" Jack said. He was trying not to cry.

She splashed over to the table and pulled them into her. "Hey," she said. "Hey, you pumpkins." They were soaked, all of them; they stank like a pond.

She pressed her nose into Aidan's head and waited for the adrenaline to stop chattering in her veins. She could have been thinking of how lucky she was (the tank could have landed on one of them; it could have shattered), or feeling guilty for leaving them alone, or trying to recall whether she'd finished everything at the barn. But she wasn't; she was coasting on a surge of relief and well-being. Everything was okay; she could still ride.

Pam drove the back way to Jack's school, taking the curves low and fast. The air coming through the window was laced with the smells of summer: new hay, warming asphalt, the secret damp of the woods. She would start Ace off with some basic dressage, she thought—halts, extensions—get him back into the mind-set. She held her hand out the window like a wing and let it fly up on the rush of air.

When she came home from the grocery store two hours later, she found Ace with his nose in the grain bin. She had forgotten to shut the paddock door.

———

That terrible night, when Pam had spotted Brian lying so strangely on the frozen ground, her mind had refused. *No* was what she thought. Not a plea or a prayer but a command: *No.*

Even as she ran to call the ambulance, even when the EMT stood up in defeat; even the next day, when she was making the funeral plans and relatives were arriving, she was secretly refusing. The blows that came after—the animals dying, the children's bewildered grief, the nightly jolt of waking and finding him gone—these were nothing some-how, or rather they were more of the same, water poured into a torrent of water. She stood there and took it.

But now her resistance deserted her. She had done this. If Ace died, if he foundered, it would be her fault alone.

He raised his head and looked at her; then he burrowed his nose back in the bin and began eating in a frenzy, flinging grain against the metal sides. She made herself step forward and grab his halter; then she jerked his head out and backed him into the aisle.

She clipped him into the crossties with shaking hands and went to get the thermometer and stethoscope. A fluttery weakness had come over her, and she leaned against him to steady herself while she took his vital signs. She had seen a lot of colic over the years but only two cases from grain: one in her first pony, the other in a dressage horse at the barn where she had trained. The horse had died when the swelling grain ruptured her intestines. The pony had survived, but afterward he had foundered—his hooves had curled back on themselves like elf shoes, and he could never be ridden again. They had kept him anyway, as a pet. You could do that with a pony.

She put Ace in his stall and took the water bucket out. Then she went back to the house to call the vet.

"Oh boy," he said. It was Leland, the younger partner, the nice one. "Any idea how much he ate?"

"No," she said. "A lot, I think."

"Pulse and everything fine?"

"So far."

"Well, get him walking and let me know how things progress." He told her his cellphone number and she wrote it on her arm. When he had hung up, she called Trish to ask if she could take the kids overnight.

"Of course," Trish said. "Oh, Pam, I'm so sorry."

"Thanks," Pam whispered. She stopped to get control of her voice. "You still have their sleeping bags, right?"

—

She walked Ace on the driveway: down to the mailbox, then back up to the house, then again. He was bright-eyed and frisky, and every time he caught sight of the other horses, he tossed his head up and whinnied. Pam looked away, sick with guilt. He didn't know what was coming. She had forgotten to change out of her riding boots and they were blistering her heels, but this seemed to her justified, so she did nothing about it.

Around two o'clock Ace started nipping his sides; by three he was trying to go down on the driveway. She put him in the paddock, where he wouldn't hurt himself if he thrashed, and went to call the vet.

She waited for Leland in the scant shade of the linden tree, watching Ace paw and turn and bite at himself. He went down and rolled, and she pulled him up by the halter—if he twisted a gut it would be all over. He stood for a while sweating, his eyes anxious; then he went down again. The dogs came by, sniffed the air, and slunk off. When the vet finally came, an hour and a half later, Pam's relief bordered on elation. But Leland's face went still when he saw the horse, and he performed the examination in silence.

"Is there an impaction?" Pam asked.

"Yes, in the colon. I'm not sure if the cecum is involved or not." Leland rubbed his jaw. "Well, we can give him mineral oil, see how that does."

Pam managed a nod. Mineral oil seemed to her a remedy from the nineteenth century, like cupping or leeches—well intentioned but useless. She held the twitch on Ace's lip while Leland slipped the tube down his throat. When he was done, she trailed him out to his truck.

He opened the door and put in his bag. "Do you have insurance on him?" he said.

She nodded. What he meant was could she afford surgery, but she knew that if it got that far, Ace's chances would be slim.

"You might want to go ahead and hook the trailer up just in case we need to take him in," Leland said. "If he hasn't passed anything by nine or he gets noticeably worse, you know, pulse over fifty, an increase in distress—"

"Sitting like a dog," she added, grimly. That was what the dressage horse had done.

Leland paused. "Well, yes, of course, if you see that," he said. He put his hand on the truck door. "So, anything changes for the worse, call the answering service and they'll page Norton."

"Oh," Pam said, "Norton."

Norton was the other vet, and he didn't like Pam. He was a homely man, with large, squarish limbs and the bitter arrogance of someone who expected to be slighted. His wife had left him, very publicly, for the local dentist a few years earlier. Pam would have felt sorry for him, but his dislike for her had been so immediate she never got the chance. When she had brought in the dead kittens, he had just raised his eyebrows and shrugged. "Congenital would be my guess," he'd said, and then he had crossed his arms and waited for her to go.

She had stood there for a moment feeling frivolous, spoiled, shallow—whatever it was he disliked her for. Then she had picked up the box of kittens and left.

"Norton's good, Pam," Leland said. "He'll do a good job."

"Oh, I know," she said. She watched his truck until it disappeared from view.

—

The hours dragged on. Dusk fell and she brought the other horses back to eat. Later, she went to the house and called the children to say good night. She made a peanut-butter sandwich but her throat was closed, and she threw it away and went back out to the paddock. Ace was standing by the fence, his head sunk. He had extended his legs in an effort to ease the pain, and this made him look swaybacked and broken, like an old nag. She went up and put a hand on his dirt-encrusted neck, but his eyes reflected no awareness of her or anything else. The horse she knew had disappeared.

She turned away, sickened. A terrible pressure was building in her head. She walked around to the back of the tree and sat down where she wouldn't have to see him. The things she had done—against nature, against her own ability even—were coming back to her. Carrying the bloody puppy. Dragging the bloated goat bodies from the pond. Stacking the dead kittens in the shoe box.

She gripped her head. She had the feeling of something cracking, of a tremendous force bearing down. What good had she been? She hadn't even been there when Brian died. And when she had gotten there— Her mind recoiled at the thought of her exaggerated gasping, her stupid fingers fumbling to get under his scarf. There was something monstrous, something treacherous and insincere about the ordinary way she had gone on functioning while Brian lay there cold. And the dumb show of running to call 911—running, when she already knew it was too late.

Ace's hooves scraped wearily against the dirt. She put her hands over her ears and shut her eyes. She didn't mean to fall asleep; she was just going to spell her eyes for a minute, but the relief of giving up was too strong. She let herself sink.

—

She was floating in a green dream, in the sleepy, droning calm of a summer afternoon. A horse took shape and went galloping, galloping, bright as a penny. *Not lame,* she thought. She could hear the hooves in slow motion, rising up and coming down on the dry, solid ground. But the rhythm was off; the hoofbeats were too far apart.

She woke with a start. It wasn't galloping she'd heard, it was Ace, rolling. She jumped up and went to pull on his halter, but he lifted only his chin; when she let go, his head flopped back into the dirt. Her watch said 11:05. She should have called the vet two hours ago.

She phoned the answering service and then she went back to the paddock and sat down in the dirt with Ace's head in her lap. Now it seemed right that it was Norton who would come—Norton, who had seen through her.

He was there in less than a half hour. She stood unsteadily when she saw him walking up along the fence. He didn't bother with a greeting, just took a stethoscope out of his bag and went straight to the horse. "How'd he get into the grain?" he said, crouching down to take the pulse.

"I had him in the paddock—I was going to ride—" she began, but it was too much effort. "I left the door open."

Norton took the stethoscope out of his ears. "And what time did you find him?" He went over everything: when the symptoms started, what Leland had given him; how he'd been since. She answered blindly, hardly knowing what she said.

"What was his pulse when you called?"

Pam flushed. In her panic she had forgotten to take it.

Suddenly Ace lurched up and sat on his haunches. Norton stiffened. The horse's ears were back and his eyes had suddenly focused, as though attending to something they couldn't see. For a long minute nothing happened. Then his back legs jerked. *Please, God,* Pam thought, but she was alone; she knew that. No one was going to help her.

The horse's legs jerked again. With tremendous effort he dragged them under himself and scrambled up. He lifted his tail.

"Here we go," Norton said.

It was the sound of the manure falling that made her understand: He was past it; he was okay.

—

She stood at the horse's head while Norton talked. Something had made him friendly—the horse's recovery or maybe just the late hour—and he was chatting away about other cases, about founder, about a prank in vet school years before. She listened in a daze, not following. She would have liked to speak, to show her gratitude, but she couldn't. The terrible knot of the day had unraveled; she had been spared. It made no sense.

When Ace had passed the rest of the impaction, Norton folded his stethoscope into his bag and clicked the clasp shut. "He should be okay," he said. "Leland will be out in the morning to check his feet again, but they seem all right now." He pointed a finger at the horse. "Next time don't eat so much," he said.

"Oh," Pam said, "there won't be a next time."

Norton slung his bag over his shoulder. "Well, everyone has to eat."

"No," she said, "no, I mean I'm going to sell him." She could feel Norton watching her. "I can't, you know, I obviously can't take care of him properly anymore. So . . ." She kept her brimming eyes focused on her hand, which was stroking the wide, flat bone of Ace's head.

"Everyone has to eat," Norton said again.

She did not understand his words; she couldn't even attach them to the conversation they were having, but, like an animal, she understood the tone. Not forgiveness, not liking, but a kind of permission. Something rushed loose in her. She listened to Norton's feet turn in the dirt, the slap of the fence boards as he ducked through. When she heard his truck door slam, she put her head against the horse's neck and sobbed.

Later she got a couple of horse blankets and lay down in the paddock where she could hear Ace. She gazed up at the dizzy, patternless sweep of the stars. Brian had died here, alone on this dirt. Her exhausted mind summoned up the shape of his body with startling clarity: the weight of his arms, the smell of his chest where her face had reached. He was gone; she would raise their children alone. She thought this; she felt the iron truth of it in her mouth, and at the same time she felt herself drifting away—into comfort and sleep, into the electric hum of her own pumping blood.

—

She woke before dawn to the silvery fluting of the wood thrushes. Ace was up, eating hay. The air was cold, but she could see that the light was coming, a bluish green band hung over the eastern hill. She threw back the blankets and stood gingerly on her blistered feet. She wanted coffee and a hot shower and an egg-and-sausage breakfast; she wanted the children back. She put her hand on Ace's neck, and he bent around to sniff her. Then she climbed stiffly through the fence and started for the house.

The valley lay quiet under the changing sky. She turned her head to take in the whole of it: the three dark hills, the broad, dim swath of the pasture; in the middle, hidden, the running stream. Soon the sun would break over the hill, morning would come. A thrill passed through her. It was Saturday. She would take the kids for a picnic, she thought, or maybe to the lake. She would get her hair cut.

She stopped at the truck, which was still parked the way she'd left it, with the horse trailer hooked up. Better to put the trailer away now, she thought, when she didn't have the children to watch. As she reached for the driver's-side door, a flicker of movement caught her eye.

Something was in there.

Warily, she put her head through the open window and squinted into the gloom. For a long moment she saw nothing. Then, in the dim light from the windshield, she caught the unmistakable gleam of an eye.

Aidan's hamster. It was sitting on the passenger side, holding one of the shrunken French fries that collected in the cracks of the seats.

Pam stood still, putting it together. It must have been Aidan, carrying it around in his pocket; he must have brought it into the car one day without her noticing, and accidentally let it go. It had been in there all this time, living off the food the kids dropped. Her eyes had adjusted, and now she saw it quite clearly: the twitching nose, the shiny, bulbous eyes. The old revulsion rose in her throat. And yet it had survived, she had to give it that.

She stared, wonder and disgust battling in her mind. Reassured by the lack of movement, the hamster raised the French fry to its mouth and began to eat.

RUTTING SEASON

Carl had a secret thought about his boss, Ray.

Ray had a secret thought about Lisa, one of the girls in fundraising.

Lisa had no thoughts about Ray, secret or otherwise. At least that's what she would have said if anyone asked her. And who would ask her? Ray just wasn't the kind of guy a girl like Lisa would think about. He was old for one thing—she put him at thirty-five, minimum—and he had the slumped shoulders and jutting forehead of a Neanderthal. Also, he was short and prone to wearing V-neck sweaters in cheap synthetic blends. If for some reason his name had come up in conversation, she would have said something like "Ray? You mean Ray the computer guy?" as though she knew a number of Rays and couldn't quite place him.

In fact, Lisa knew exactly who Ray was. She had inadvertently been the cause of a long-running joke about him. Once, at an office party, Ray had gotten drunk and stared so closely at Lisa's cleavage that his face practically touched the scoop of her scoop-neck bodysuit. In the bathroom afterward, when Lisa recounted the incident to a handful of co-workers, Lauren had wrinkled her nose and exclaimed, "Eeew! A booby gazer!"

After that, whenever the database went down or the printer wouldn't work one of them would say, "Better call Booby Gazer," and they would throw their heads back and laugh. They always pronounced it in the Boston way: "Booby Gayzah," although none of them actually spoke like that. Over time the nickname had morphed, first into "Bobby Gayzah," then, after a number of months, into "Bobby."

"Why does everyone call me Bobby?" Ray asked one day. He was standing in the hallway, looking back at them with the meek, bemused expression Lisa had sometimes seen on her father's face when she and her sisters mocked him. She felt sorry then and a little ashamed, and she pretended to be busy with a file on her desk while Lauren said, in a bright, false voice, "That's not your name?"

These two incidents were the exception, though; most days Ray never crossed Lisa's mind. So it was a surprise one morning when she woke up to find that she'd dreamed about him.

In the dream, Ray had a daughter. That was it, that was the whole dream: the fact of the daughter (she was about five or six years old), and a sweet, floating sense of joy—Ray's joy—for he had been beside himself with happiness.

"Yeah, right," Lisa said out loud, throwing off the covers. The floor was cold under her feet but the air was warm, an early-summer sensation. She stopped to stretch, naked, in front of the mirror and her breasts rose up a little, nipples erect. She stood there a moment on the cool floor, transfixed by the perfect wholeness of her reflected body. A nameless anticipation was blossoming inside her. The dullness, the shrinking withdrawal of the winter months, was over; she felt dilated and alive, like a flower tilting to meet the sun.

Out of nowhere she thought of the VP of fundraising, the corded muscles of his forearms when he rolled up his sleeves. Not that this meant anything. He was married, he had two children; there was no way she'd go down that path. The thought was just an extension of the physical happiness she felt right then, of the heightened sense of perception that brought to her, as she dropped her arms and walked into the bathroom, the memory of his smell—sharp and slightly sour beneath the starch of his shirt.

—

Lisa had no intention of mentioning her dream to Ray. Why on earth would she? It was weird enough that she'd dreamed it. Later that day, though, when she saw him sit down alone at the other end of the office lunchroom, she heard herself call out, "Hey, Ray, I dreamt you had a daughter."

Ray looked up from his sub. "A daughter?" he said, his face oddly empty of expression. "Really?"

"Yeah," Lisa said carelessly, "a little girl, like about five years old."

Ray tipped his head. "A daughter," he said. A quizzical, wondering look came into his eyes.

Then Ray's assistant, Carl, lumbered in with a slice of pizza on a paper plate and Ray's expression darkened. "You better not be coming in here if that server's not backed up," he said.

Carl bent his head like a balky ox. "I'm not," he muttered.

Ray glanced at Lisa and snorted. "What do you mean you're not? You're not in here?"

"Th-th-the backup's already f-finished." Carl's face had turned the dark red of an internal organ.

Lisa stabbed a piece of lettuce with her fork. Why do that? Why make the guy stutter? So Carl was a weirdo—that was still no reason to humiliate him. Ray really was a dick; she was sorry now she'd bothered to say anything to him. She took a few more bites of her salad and read another paragraph in her magazine, just to show that she had nothing to do with either of them. Then she closed the lid of the plastic container, tucked the magazine under her arm, and walked out of the room.

She was aware, without actually thinking about it, of the figure she cut from behind: the curve of her skirt (her butt was one of her best features), the swing of her long, dark hair. It was not that Ray and Carl were men she wanted to attract; it was just a habit, like checking the rearview mirror in the car. She was used to being noticed and she dressed for it.

Down the hall in the kitchen, she dumped out the remains of her salad and put her fork and glass in the sink. Someone, or maybe several people, had left their dirty dishes: a few mugs, a plate, a glass filled with used silverware. Lisa squirted soap on the sponge and slowly, without resentment, began to wash them.

At the beginning, when she was thirteen and just developing, being stared at had humiliated her. Men seemed to watch her everywhere—when she bought a Slushee at the convenience store, while she waited at the bus stop. She would feel it before she saw it: the tensing of the air, the sudden, blood-freezing isolation of being marked out. Then a hot shame would claim her body and she would hunch her shoulders and hurry by. No one ever helped her. When it happened once at the post office, her mother just turned away, a rigid half smile on her lips, and asked for two books of stamps.

Over time, this fear and confusion had subsided. Being attractive became a part of Lisa's sense of herself, something she could flaunt (in a white halter top and mini) or pretend to disregard (sweatshirt and baseball hat). This public Lisa was her, but also was not; she held it out at a little distance from herself, like one of those old-fashioned masks on a stick.

It was a relief, at times like this, to forget all that, to let the sound of the running water, the warm sun from the kitchen window, lull her into silence. An animal silence, without any need to think or react or monitor, the clamoring, unruly thing she knew as herself suspended, batlike, in a corner.

She laid a clean paper towel on the counter and then, with a simple sense of pleasure, placed on it the clean forks and spoons, the mugs and glass, the plate.

—

That night Carl woke in a sweat, his blood pounding. He sat up and reached into the drawer of his bedside table, crawling his thick fingers past the magazines until they made contact with the cold steel of his grandfather's gun. The red numbers on the clock read 4:08. He pulled his hand back and lay down again. *Go to sleep,* he told himself, but it was too late, he was already thinking about Ray.

What do you mean you're not? You're not in here? And then stupid him, stuttering like an idiot in front of that hot girl from the fundraising department. Lisa, her name was. They were all like that in fundraising, stalking around in their high boots, swishing their hair. They didn't give Carl the time of day. Or Ray either, for that matter. For a second this thought eased the tightness in Carl's chest. But then he started thinking of other things Ray had said, days and weeks and months of things. *You didn't know that, Carl? You haven't finished that, Carl? Carl, Carl, Carl.* He would come and stand in the doorway and say that, loud enough for everyone on the hall to hear: *Carl, Carl, Carl.* A sort of joke it was supposed to be, one guy ribbing another. No one but Carl saw the hard edge of contempt in Ray's eyes.

During the day, when they happened, Carl's impression of these incidents was muffled and oblique, as though he were listening through a heavy scarf. Even the adrenaline that surged through him at those moments had a distant, barely felt quality. One or two nights a week, though, Carl would lurch out of sleep, his body tense with fury. Then it all would come back to him with searing precision, and he would lie awake reliving every insult.

The gun added a new dimension. Carl had acquired it accidentally a few months earlier, at the estate sale at his grandfather's house. The morning before the sale, everyone in the family had gone to the house to pick something out for themselves. They were given colored stickers and told to tag whatever they wanted. Carl chose his grandfather's bedroom set. This hadn't seemed strange to him; he'd just moved to a new apartment and he needed a bed. The matching bedside tables and dresser were an afterthought: They all went together, so it seemed like a smart decision to tag them, too. But his father had made a big deal out of it afterward with his uncles. What kind of a douche bag would ask for a dresser when he could get a rifle or a table saw? Carl's father looked around at his brothers as he spoke, the laughter already beginning to shake in his loose, red cheeks. He turned one hand palm up, as if to say, "Are you with me or what?"

They were, of course. Or so Carl assumed. He kept his face averted, so he never actually saw who had joined in and who hadn't.

It was only after he got home that he found the gun, as he was idly pulling open the drawers of one of the side tables. It was in the top drawer, wedged behind a piece of cardboard that made a false back a few inches from the real one. Taped down beside it was a small box of bullets. Carl picked up the gun and turned it over slowly in his large hands. It was as small and flat as the water pistols he had played with as a child, but surprisingly heavy. In an indented circle above the handle was an Indian chief and around it, in old-fashioned typeface, the words SAVAGE QUALITY.

What Carl felt, holding his grandfather's gun, was the boyish elation of a lucky find. It was only later that the gun became mixed up with the things he thought about when he woke in the night.

At first, what he imagined was Ray's face—how his expression would change when he saw the gun. *Carl, Carl, Carl . . .* and then what? Carl envisioned a hundred different scenarios: Ray falling to his knees, Ray begging and blubbering, Ray crapping his pants. These were all good, but after a while Carl needed more. He needed to see Ray hurt; he needed to know that Ray couldn't just get up off the floor and go back to being Ray. Slowly, the scenes Carl imagined shifted from threats to actual violence—beating on Ray's face with the butt of the gun, kicking him; even, finally, shooting him.

But here the pure jet of Carl's rage always shut off. The thrill of cutting Ray down to size would evaporate and a panicky, lost feeling would take its place. Carl would start worrying about logistics: how to get out of the building, and whether he'd be able to arrange a getaway car, and how to get to Mexico, and also, on particularly bad days, who else he might have to shoot.

Tonight what he was thinking about was Lisa: Would he have to kill her, too? He saw again the disdain in her face as she turned back to her salad, and flushed. It was always like that with girls for him—it was always no, and forget about it, and what do you think you're looking at?

He lay in the dark, eyes closed, imagining what Lisa would say when she saw the gun. Would she beg? Scream? Offer him a blow job? That was an interesting train of thought, but soon he was distracted by the question of how he would get to her desk before the cops came, because he'd have to do Ray first, that was a given.

He tried to picture the fundraising area. Was her desk the one by the VP's office? Or was it at the other end of the row of cubicles, by the watercooler? And what if she wasn't at her desk; would he have to run around looking for her? After a while, without Carl's noticing, his thoughts became magical and confused, until he and Lisa were together in a swimming pool, naked and smooth and wonderfully warm. She pulled him close and he put his arms around her, his hands clasping the two ends of the gun behind the small of her back. Lisa leaned in and whispered, "I can drive you." She had the car running already, he could hear its horn beeping rhythmically in the background. Relief washed through him. Only why did she have to keep shoving his shoulder like that?

Carl woke with a jolt to find his roommate shaking him. The alarm on the digital clock was going off.

"Carl! Jesus Christ, are you deaf? That thing's been beeping for, like, ten minutes already."

"Sorry," Carl mumbled as he reached over to hit the button. The sound cut off. 8:05. Too late for anything but a quick change of clothes. He leaned back against the headboard and waited for his startled heart to slow.

Usually, in the daylight, Carl's idea—the idea of killing anyone—seemed nightmarish and absurd. But this morning, after he had put on his coat and shut the apartment door, he stood in the hallway for a minute. He felt weak-kneed and shaky, as though he'd just been bested in a fight. He wasn't up to a day of work; even the idea of getting on the bus felt vaguely threatening. And of course when he got there Ray would be all over him because this time he *was* going to be late; there was nothing he could do about that now.

Staring at the battered metal doorknob, Carl felt the cage of his life close around him. Quickly, before he could change his mind, he went back into the apartment and fished the gun out of the drawer.

—

Ray had a dream of his own. He dreamed about a puppy. Or maybe was it a lobster? It was hard to tell. He held it in the crook of his arm and its warmth spread through his chest. Later, when it was definitely a puppy, he took it for a walk through the mall. But then he realized he shouldn't have—it was too weird-looking, with that red shell, those little ball eyes sticking up on their stems; it just didn't look like a puppy should look. He thought about maybe ditching it, opening one of the exit doors and unclipping the leash, giving it a little shove. But it broke his heart to think that, so he went on walking, stiff with shame.

Then a miraculous shift occurred. A young girl pointed at the lobster dog and cried, "How cute!" She came over; she bent down and patted the dog on its hard, red head. Other people stopped, too: teenage girls, mothers with baby strollers, other men. Everyone was friendly; everyone seemed to like Ray. They leaned toward him, smiling, and Ray smiled back. A weight seemed to lift off him; when he half-woke and rolled over, the bed felt softer.

He was still in a good mood when he got up in the morning. He flung back witty comments at the men on the morning talk show; he even thought, shaving, that his face looked a little chiseled—*GQ*-ish, even, from a certain angle. Outside, the warm spring air held a scent of flowers. He threw his keys up in the air and caught them, just for the hell of it.

But when he turned the key in the car's ignition and heard the frantic, failing whinny of the starter, the mess of everything rose up before him again: things done wrong (leaving the headlights on, the new fundraising database) or still unsolved (the email server), or just not happening (sex, love, money—you name it), and then something else that had been nagging at the back of his mind, a problem from the day before. It didn't come to him until later, while he was waiting for the AAA truck: Lisa in the lunchroom, the look on her face when Carl came in. No, not when Carl came in—it was after Ray spoke to Carl. It was Ray she'd been looking at when her eyes went hard.

Ray spread his hands out against the steering wheel and stared at the coarse black hairs on the backs of his fingers. Why had he spoken to Carl anyway? He hadn't wanted to talk to Carl; hell, he hadn't even wanted him in the room. What Lisa had said about her dream had brought about some change in the atmosphere: a thaw, a little opening. Sitting there, talking with her alone like that, he'd felt as though he might be on the verge of something. Then Carl showed up. Carl, with his big, reluctant body, his drawling *Um, yeah.* Did you run the backup, Carl? *Um, yeah.* Is the email server down again, Carl? *Um, yeah.* Could you get a fuckin' clue, Carl? *Um, yeah.*

Ray had tried with Carl; no one could say he hadn't. He'd sent him to classes, suggested books to read. He tried to be a mentor, he really did—he gave Carl pointers on a daily basis. But nothing seemed to get through: Carl's large, slack face remained a stubborn blank. Just the way he moved was enough to drive a person crazy, just the way he dragged his feet over the carpet, as though the entire gravitational force of the earth was pulling on him. And underneath, concealed by that expressionless face of his, a sneaky undercurrent of rebellion, of disrespect.

But Lisa had not seen any of that. All Lisa had seen was Ray, and what she had seen had disgusted her. A spasm of anger ran through him. He got out of the car and slammed the door. Where the hell was AAA?

—

When Ray stopped at Dunkin' Donuts in the morning, he usually drank his coffee in his car in the office parking lot. That way he could listen to the radio and also avoid looking cheap for not picking up extras the way the VP of fundraising always did. But today, by the time the tow truck showed up and the car had been jumped, he was running nearly an hour late. He'd have to take his coffee into the office like everyone else. He barked his order at the Indian girl behind the register, put the exact change on the counter, and watched, irritated, as she carefully took a cup off the stack and filled it with coffee. She placed the lid on the cup and pressed around its entire circumference with one slender brown finger. *For chrissake!* Ray thought. It was ridiculous to have someone so slow on the morning shift. He had just decided to complain about her to the manager when the girl looked up at him and smiled. Not a fake smile but a real one: Her whole face lit up.

"There you are," she said in her musical accent.

Ray took the cup from her outstretched hand. "Thank you," he said stiffly. His tone was harsher than he'd intended, and as he turned away he saw the smile die on her face. He walked heavily toward the door. Through the glass, he could see the bright spring light glittering on the cars, a triangle of blue sky, but these seemed as far away as the happiness he had felt earlier, something for other people to enjoy.

He spotted the girl the instant he turned around, shining like a beacon between the backs of the people in line. He took his place behind a construction worker and waited. "You know what?" he said in a friendlier voice when he reached the counter, again, "I think I'll take another one."

He was rewarded with another smile. "Most certainly," the girl said. "How would you like that?"

Ray had turned around on instinct; he hadn't actually decided who the extra coffee should be for. *Lisa,* he thought, but then he remembered he was in trouble with Lisa; also, that he'd only ever seen her drinking tea. This brought him to Carl. Grudgingly, he let himself think it: The coffee should be for Carl. Bring the guy a coffee; show Lisa that he wasn't whatever she'd thought he was back in the lunchroom yesterday. Ray pictured the half-drunk coffee Carl abandoned on his desk every day, the milky star on its surface. "Light," he told the girl, "and I think no sugar."

"Light, no sugar," she repeated.

It was the right thing to do, he could tell, because immediately he felt better. He took the two coffees and pushed open the glass door with his shoulder, his shoes crunching on the leftover winter sand by the curb. When he turned the key, the engine started right up.

—

Carl was sitting at his desk with his jacket on. His head was buzzing with exhaustion, or maybe hunger? He had skipped breakfast to make the bus. And now Ray wasn't even there. A fresh wave of anger washed through him at this thought, and he pictured Ray again: Ray sneering, Ray gloating, Ray in the doorway saying his name. He reached into his coat and touched the gun. The cold metal seemed to transmit a shock. Was this it? Was he really going to do it?

This was the trouble with bringing a gun to work: You couldn't stop thinking about it. Shoot Ray, don't shoot Ray, shoot Ray—he'd been back and forth at least ten times already. He flipped the safety off and then on again, staring at the small patch of carpet between his feet.

To the extent Carl had ever thought of the carpet, he'd thought of it as gray; now, though, he saw that it was a random mixture of colors—there were brown parts in it and even black. His eyes traced a strange, H-shaped group of brown nubs; then an anomalous patch of white. There was no pattern to it, really; in fact, he could see it was kind of a mess now that he looked at it. Still, it felt surprisingly good to sit there and stare. The office was quiet. No one walked past; even the hum of the servers was strangely muted. He seemed to be alone in a little bubble of timelessness. Slowly he let his eyes drift out of focus.

Time stretched out, a vast, featureless plain, then suddenly shrank to nothing: Ray was coming heavily down the hall. The door to his office opened and then shut, shaking the cheaply made walls. For a few moments there was no sound. Then Carl heard Ray's door open again. Heat flashed through him. *This is it,* he thought. A quick glance at the monitor was all Ray would need to see that he hadn't done any of the morning tasks. For once Carl deserved to be yelled at. He kept his eyes on the carpet. He sensed, rather than saw, that Ray had come to stand in the doorway.

"Carl, Carl, Carl," Ray said.

Inside his coat pocket, Carl flipped off the safety.

Still moping, Ray thought. He held out the cup. "I stopped by Dunkin' Donuts," he said. But Carl didn't look up; he was staring at the floor in the sullen, beast-of-burden way that drove Ray nuts.

Carl could feel his hand holding the gun, far away at the end of his arm. *Now,* he thought, *I could do it now.* Blood began to hammer in his head.

"Got you a coffee," Ray said.

Coffee. The word snagged in Carl's mind.

Ray stuck his arm out a little farther. "I stopped at Dunkin' Donuts."

Dimly, Carl registered the repetition, the outthrust cup. Now here was a situation: Ray was sucking up to him. Or was this just a new way of dicking him around? His heart was so loud he couldn't think. He adjusted his grip on the gun, waiting for a cue.

What happened next was something unexpected: There was a noise in the hallway, the brisk slap-slap-slap of someone walking in flip-flops.

"Oh, hey there!" Ray called out. "Good morning!"

There was something in his voice—a softness or even a pleading—that made Carl glance up. With a little shock of pleasure, he recognized Lisa's dark head.

"Keepin' busy, huh?" Ray said.

"Yep," Lisa said, not bothering to look at him.

"What is it, crunch time for the annual?"

Carl could still see Lisa; she was just a few feet beyond Ray. It wasn't possible that she hadn't heard his question. And yet she kept walking, she turned the corner into the copy room with the end of her ponytail bouncing against her slender back.

Ray stared after her. "Annual appeal," he said. "Lot of pressure on those girls."

But nothing he said could cover for it: Carl had seen how

she had treated him. The Ray who turned back toward him now, the Ray who stood in the doorway, his hand on the sill, was a different Ray—a blunted, weakened Ray. Carl let his eyes drop back to the rug.

"Anyway, here you go," Ray said, holding the cup out again. "Light, no sugar, right?"

It came to Carl that he could just reach out and take it. He could let go of the gun and take the coffee, and all the ordinariness, the familiar nothingness of the rug, would remain as it was. He would not have to kill anyone, he would not have to run. He would not have to hunt Lisa down in the fundraising department.

In the doorway, Ray felt his eyes snap with irritation. The tension in his jaw was coming back. He forced himself to try again. "What, that's not how you take it?" he said.

Carl scanned the muddle of gray and brown nubs, hesitating. He was forgetting something, something important. A pull like that of a still-warm bed, a promise—of sex or skin; a warm, naked tangling. He blinked, unable to remember. A fantasy, it must have been, or a dream; something that had no place in the cold fluorescent light of the office. Slowly, as though he were waking from a trance, Carl raised his eyes. "No. No, I mean—yeah. That's how I take it. Light. No sugar." He pulled his large hand out of his coat and took the cup.

"Okay, good," Ray said. He let his breath out, inexplicably relieved. "Good," he said again, as he stepped backward into the hall.

Carl held the cup with both hands. He could smell it now: the bitter coffee, the faint underlying sweetness of the cream. Ray's head reappeared in the doorway. "Hey, ahh, don't forget we've got that meeting on the new database at eleven. Should be a real ballbuster."

"Yeah, I know," Carl said. "Thanks," he added, but Ray was already gone.

—

Walking back down the hallway with her copies, Lisa caught a glimpse of Carl through the open door, his head bent. He seemed to be cradling something in his hands. She froze in midstep, alarmed. She had the odd impression it was something alive—a bird maybe, or a mouse. But when she glanced back, she spotted the familiar pink and orange logo between his fingers. It was only a cup of coffee; he was just trying to wake up, the poor slob.

WHAT IT TAKES

Sylvie was a new friend that fall, a rarity in the static world of our neighborhood, where most of us had known each other since kindergarten. She wasn't the kind of person we normally hung out with. She loved the Grateful Dead, a band we prided ourselves on despising, and she dressed in ratty jeans and crinkled skirts, like a hippie from the sixties. The way she talked was straight out of the sixties, too. Everything was "cool" or "groovy" or "wild," words I associated with the aging burnouts who hung around on the Green downtown.

For some reason, I overlooked all that. We all did—even Robert, with his fanatical devotion to New Wave. With Sylvie, those kinds of social distinctions seemed narrow-minded and petty. It was like she was above all that, like the long, mysterious trail of her experience had given her a wisdom we could only guess at. She'd done everything: hitchhiked to California, smoked heroin, run away to follow the Dead. She was only in our high school that fall because she'd been kicked out of boarding school again, the second in three years.

I had begun to feel, that year, that the sameness of every-thing was choking me to death: the suffocating familiarity of my mother's house; the constant sense of menace at school; the city of New Haven itself, with its shuttered factories and listless, dated stores.

Sylvie seemed like the perfect antidote. "You gotta do your own thing," she'd say. Or, "You're alive *today,* man." Or her favorite: "It's all cool." She made it seem like you didn't have to do the same stuff everyone else did. Like you could make up your own rules, invent something better, and anyone who said you couldn't was just a loser and a drag.

—

In the afternoons, when we were free, Sylvie and James and Robert and I would walk downtown to Clark's Dairy. The food wasn't very good, but there was something comforting about cramming into a booth together after the long, fraught hours at school.

One day, as we were sharing a single order of fries in the back, Robert announced, "So these guys at school tried to jump me."

I glanced over to gauge Sylvie's reaction. I never told anyone when I got harassed at school, especially not Sylvie, but her face was expressionless behind the coiling smoke of her cigarette.

"Big guys," Robert went on, "with those stockings on their heads, you know? For when they put that stuff in their hair? What's it called?"

"Jheri curl," I said.

"Right, Jheri curl." Robert picked up a few fries and brushed their limp ends through the puddle of ketchup.

"So . . . ?" James made a wheel motion with his hand, like "get on with it."

"Well, actually, that was highly relevant," Robert said. "I mean, how seriously can you take a guy with a nude knee-high on his head?"

Sylvie snorted.

It had started in the usual way: He was walking down the hall, minding his own business, when suddenly the stocking-head guys stepped out of the crowd and pushed him into an alcove. They trash-talked him for a minute and then they shoved him against the wall—the typical prelude. This time, though, Robert had an inspiration: He curled up his lip and started to growl.

He leaned over the green Formica table to show us how he'd done it: growl, lunge, bark, growl—basically an imitation of the performance his dog Pepe put on for the mailman every afternoon. The growling made the two guys hesitate. What stopped them, though, was the drool, a long string of it that Robert let stretch down from the corner of his mouth.

"You should have seen them back up," he crowed. He mimicked the high-pitched tone the black kids in our school used for emphasis, "'I ain't touching that rabies shit! I ain't touching that rabies shit!'"

James hooted, slapping the table with his hands. Even Sylvie was smiling. I bent my head to hide the sour expression I could feel on my face. Robert was our nerdy version of cool: brainy, black-clad, always up on the latest records from the Gang of Four and the Talking Heads and other bands I'd never even heard of. But I was cool, too, cooler than him in some ways, if you factored in that I was a girl. When he bought pot, he bought it from me. So why couldn't I get the better of those kids? Why couldn't I win for once?

"Rabies shit," Sylvie said, shaking her head, the trace of a smile still bending her lips.

She took a drag on her cigarette and my eyes followed the fine, curved edge of her jaw. Sylvie was a perfect harmony of colors: blue-blue eyes, summer blond hair, even the startling pink of her mouth was just right. But all that was like a landscape seen through a chain-link fence because nothing about the way she moved or talked was beautiful. Her walk was a boy's walk, slouch-shouldered and bouncy, and she held her cigarettes overhand, like the Marlboro Man. I watched her stub out the butt in the leftover ketchup, a familiar anxiety stealing over me.

The waitress came up and stood at the end of our booth, her arms folded beneath the mound of her chest. "Gonna need the table," she said. It was a lie, nearly all the tables were empty, but we knew there was no point in arguing.

James winked at me. "Okay, people," he said, flipping his long bangs off his forehead, "let's get the woman some cold, hard cash." He reached into his pocket and dumped a handful of change on the table.

I dug around the roll of bills I had from dealing and pulled up some quarters to add to the pile. James counted the coins beneath the waitress's reddening face. Then, with little flourishes of his fingers, he began to stack them by denomination: quarters, nickels, dimes.

"Oh, for chrissake," the waitress muttered, lunging forward to rake the money off the table. "You think it's all fun and games, don't you? One big joke." She glared around the table at us. "You wait. You just wait."

We watched her waddle off on her thick, crooked feet. Adults were always saying stuff like that to us: *You wait. You'll see,* like they already knew how things were going to turn out. Even the nice ones, the ones who took the trouble to ask us what we were interested in or where we wanted to go to college, seemed secretly doubtful. "Oh, interesting!" they'd say, a little too brightly, their eyes carefully vacant, like shoppers who'd already decided not to buy.

I walked to the bus stop with Sylvie, kicking at whatever loose stuff lay in my path. Robert's little triumph had left me feeling bad in the way I often did—worried and dissatisfied and wanting. I felt like the world was closed to me; like in some secret, irrevocable way, I didn't have what it took.

Sylvie shook out another cigarette. "Wild about Robert, huh?"

"I guess," I said, kicking at a bottle cap. It skittered a few short inches and stuck in a crack.

"Acting like a crazy man." She meant it as a compliment, I could tell.

—

The situation at our high school came down to a few basic stats: (1) Eighty percent of the students were black; (2) nearly half of the student body—over seven hundred kids—would drop out before graduation; (3) only a handful would go on to college; (4) the vast majority of that handful would be us.

We were the children of the city's doctors and lawyers and Yale professors, and we lived in a pretty, tree-lined area near East Rock Park. The school was located a few blocks away, between our neighborhood and the small, worn homes where the other white kids lived. Most of the black kids lived in a blighted area on the other side of Prospect Hill. To get to school, they had to walk nearly a mile: up the hill and then down again, past our tranquil lawns and large, well-kept houses.

Naturally, they got their revenge. They took our back-packs, they shoved us against the lockers, they slapped us and slugged us and called out threats and insults through the school's grime-streaked, fifties-era windows. We were "Freaks" or "Brainiacs," "stuck up" or "sorry"; we were whatever they said we were, and then we had to pay for it.

The black boys were tough and they went for the sexual thing right away, like that was all we were good for anyway, but it was the girls we really feared. They would come after us for anything: for accidentally stepping on their shoes or answering back or failing to answer back or just for walking down the hall with an expression on our faces. They went from indifference to rage in a flash, and they fought without rules—kicking and scratching and flailing their arms. Once, in the courtyard, I'd seen one girl rip another's earring right through her lobe.

None of this was a mystery. We had liberal parents, we knew about civil rights and slavery and segregated lunch counters. That was part of why they'd sent us to public school: to show how now, in the enlightened 1980s, we finally knew better. Fine, whatever. To me, ideas like that had nothing to do with the experience of being in that school. That was just about being hated, and being hated is just about you: your fear, your humiliation, the cowardly stink of yourself and your own pathetic desire to survive.

I wanted to fight back; I didn't want to pretend I didn't hear their insults or stand there and let them work me over like the Brainiac girls did. But there was a fierceness in them, a merciless fury that completely outmatched anything I could summon up. I didn't hit them back; I didn't even run. I stood there and let them do whatever they felt like doing.

Fight! Fight! A nigger and a white! Everyone said it, the black kids and the white kids both. Chanting it together as they crowded in to watch, like it was the one thing they could all agree on.

—

I liked selling pot. I liked the money, and the status it gave me, and the weirdly satisfying process of weighing and bagging and rolling joints. And I'd gotten used to the constant, low-grade worry about being caught, or selling to the wrong person, or having my mom find my stash. That September, though, dealing started to cause me trouble at school. For some dickhead reason of his own, the guy I bought from suddenly decided that he'd only sell to me on Mondays, between 11:30 and 12:00. That was fourth period, Phys Ed. It didn't matter if I missed it; the problem was getting in and out of the school. One of the teachers had been fatally shot near the lunchroom the year before and now all the doors were either locked or manned by security guards. There was only one exception that I knew of, a side door across from the park that had a broken lock. I came up with a new routine: slip out the broken door at the fourth-period bell, run across the park to the dealer's house to buy my quarter, dash home and hide it in my room. Then, if I had time, I'd make a quick sandwich (like that's why I was home) before I snuck back through the door for fifth-period Trig.

After a couple of weeks, I had it down to a drill. Then one Monday, as I rounded the stair landing, I saw that the side door was already open. A knot of black faces turned and looked up at me from the bottom of the stairwell. They were guys I'd never seen before, from Voc Ed maybe; five of them—four smallish, one big. I felt my heart double-clutch.

They watched me walk down the last flight of stairs— watching but that was all. No one moved or said anything, and it crossed my mind that it could be okay, it could be one of those unexpected little moments of truce when they laughed or said, "What's up?" or just moved out of the way. Three steps from the door, two steps from the door—I had my hand against the sill and was stepping outside when one of the small ones reached for my chest. A halfhearted grab, like he was just trying it out, but a bolt of fear shot through me.

"Get off!" I squeaked, twisting out of the way.

The boy's mocking, half-curious expression hardened into hostility. He moved toward me, eyes narrowed. "What you say, girl?"

They were all bunched up together in the doorway, their faces set with anger. I thought they were going to come after me—I was already out on the sidewalk by then—and for a second my knees seemed on the verge of dissolving.

One of them spat on the step. "She think she too good," he

said. Then the others started in: "You think you too good?" "Huh?" "You a dog anyway."

I turned away and walked across the street, my legs shaking.

The next week they were there again and it was *hey baby hey baby* and the rest of that crap. It had turned into the thing it always turned into: the stupid, get-something-off-a-white-girl thing.

So big deal, right? I knew they probably wouldn't hurt me, at least not in any serious, physical way. It was the feeling of it that got to me; it was coming down those stairs every Monday and having that cliff of fear rear up in my chest, and knowing I wouldn't have the guts to fight back. Afterward, walking across the park, I would be filled with a suffocating anger and if my mother came downstairs to say hello while I was making lunch, I was venomous to her.

—

"Casey, you doing this college shit?" Sylvie asked one morning, as we sat on the swings before school.

I looked into her eyes—a shock of blue—and ducked my head over the joint I was rolling. I knew why she said it that way. Already the Brainiacs were in a frenzy about their college applications: who was applying to Harvard; who was applying to Yale; who had scored what on their SATs. I had a stack of applications in the drawer of my desk at home, but that was as far as I'd gotten. The idea of college was a blank to me.

I licked the rolling paper and smoothed the seam down with my thumbs. "I don't know," I said. "Maybe. You?"

"Me," she said belligerently. She leaned back on the swing and let her hair drag in the dirty hollow everyone's feet had dug. "Me, me, me."

I didn't know what she meant by that, so I lit the joint and took a toke, thinking briefly, as always, of the inside of my grandmother's hope chest—that woodsy smell; the hollow, rectangular feeling of my straining lungs.

Sylvie sat up and took the joint from my outstretched hand. "It's just such fuckin' bullshit," she said. "You know?"

I stubbed my Doc Martens in the dirt and waited. I was often afflicted by such silences with Sylvie. The tangle of possible wrong moves would grow so thick in me I couldn't think.

"I mean, we already *did* that shit," she said.

"No shit," I said.

She took another hit and held the joint away like a cigarette. She had a tendency to bogart that I would never have tolerated in my other friends. "Life's the real teacher, you know?" she said. "I mean, think of all the amazing shit there is to do in the world."

What amazing shit? I didn't have a clue, but the idea went glinting through my brain. Looking at the cracked and netless tennis courts, I flashed on my mother, the Wellesley

graduate, drinking her days away in the gloom of her bedroom. Maybe Sylvie was right. Maybe going to college wasn't
the answer. Maybe it was better to do something totally different, something your parents hadn't even dreamed of.

It was October by then and Sylvie and I were spending
nearly all our waking hours together. When school let out,
we'd go to Clark's with James and Robert, or take off by
ourselves to smoke pot in Brewster Park. Most nights she
was over at my house, eating Stouffer's frozen dinners with
me and my mom. Afterward, we'd hang out in my bedroom
listening to *Court and Spark* and *John Barleycorn Must Die*
and talking about Sylvie's trip cross-country—what she was
going to do instead of college. After a while, she started saying
"we": When *we* go cross-country. When *we* get to California.

She thought a Volkswagen would be good. Not a bug
but one of the old minivans, with a pop-up roof. We could
learn to fix it ourselves. "You know, like *Zen and the Art of
Motorcycle Maintenance,*" she said. She was lying across my
bed staring up at the ceiling, her hair fanned out around her.

"That could be cool," I said, drawing my feet up a little
so I wouldn't touch her by mistake.

We would skip the South—who cared about all that
plantation crap?—and drive as fast as we could across the
boring Midwest. The part of the country we wanted to see
started with Colorado because Sylvie's ex-boyfriend had
told her the Rockies were an amazing place to trip. Utah
was on the list for the rock formations, and New Mexico

because it was so spiritual with all the Native Americans and everything. San Francisco—the best place—was where we would settle down.

We never looked at a map or read a travel book; our ideas about what to see came from movies and rock songs and stories we'd heard. I wasn't even sure where all those places were, what was close to what. It didn't matter. When I sat with Sylvie in my room at night, a crazy happiness brimmed up in me.

I didn't even mind my mother so much when Sylvie was around. The first night she was over, my mother wandered up in her bathrobe, drink in hand, and stood rambling irrelevantly in the door of my bedroom. I kept glancing at Sylvie as my mother stumbled through her monologue, veering from what she imagined were standard nice mother comments ("Well, we've certainly enjoyed having your family for neighbors"), to bitter jabs at my father, whom Sylvie had never met.

"Sure, Mrs. Wainwright," Sylvie said, flicking her ash into her water glass, "I can see that."

I looked away, unable to withstand the sight of my mother's penciled eyebrows or the wedge of pale, freckled skin in the V of her robe.

"Gin and tonic, huh?" Sylvie said when she had left. Then, without waiting for an answer: "That's cool, man."

—

57

I didn't see much of Sylvie at school. She'd been put in a lower track because of her bad grades, so the only class we had together was homeroom. It was a strange one, down in the Voc Ed part of the school, where neither of us had any other classes. The room didn't look like a classroom—there were no desks, just large, low tables where eight or ten students could sit—and the teacher, Mrs. Handy, didn't look like a teacher. She was black, for one thing—most of our teachers were white—and she was old. The dresses she wore were calf-length and old-fashioned, and if you got up close you could see the milky blue rings around her irises. What she looked like, actually, was one of those old ladies you'd see coming out of the churches in the black neighborhood on Sunday, with a matching hat and dress and swollen feet shoved into a pair of pumps.

I don't know what she taught—Home Ec, probably, judging by the ragged pattern books that lay around the room—it was hard to imagine her teaching anything, really. She almost never spoke, even when one of the kids started cutting up; she just sat there, outraged and silent, until the twenty-minute period was over. It was pretty clear she had given up, and that marked her as an easy target, someone we could trick and slip things past. Still, I had a funny feeling about Mrs. Handy, like I'd somehow done her wrong.

One morning, Sylvie and I stayed too long at the swings and missed the first bell. We ran all the way from the main entrance but we were still late—the final bell cut off just before we walked through the homeroom door. Another kid, one of the black guys who sat at the back of the room, came in right on our heels. I glanced at Mrs. Handy to see if she was going to bust us, but her head was bent over the newspaper. I was already seated and taking out my school-issue copy of *Dubliners* when I realized she was speaking. She had stood up behind her desk and was pointing in our direction with one bent, arthritic finger.

"You are late," she called out in her shaky, old voice. "You need to get a late pass."

I felt myself go red. "Me?" I said.

But she wasn't looking at me. She was looking past me, at the black kid who had come in with us.

His eyes widened in disbelief. "You talkin' to *me*, Ms. Handy?"

"Yes, young man, I am speaking to you. You have got to go and get yourself a late pass."

He was one of the popular boys, a basketball player, not the type to look for trouble. Game days, he came to school in a button-down shirt and tie. I turned back around and kept my eyes on the table, but Sylvie was still twisted in her chair, staring.

He started in with the charm defense: "Ms. Handy, why you gotta do me like that? You know I don't mean no disrespect. Ms. Handy, I'm askin' you. Ms. Handy!"

But Mrs. Handy had snapped; she wasn't listening to any of it. "Don't you sass me, young man!" she erupted. "Don't you sass me!"

When she threatened to call the basketball coach, I heard the boy's chair scrape the floor. He stopped at the door and looked back, his face grave. "What about them?" he said quietly, jerking his chin in our direction. "You gonna send them, too?"

"Get out!" Mrs. Handy yelled. "And take off that hat!"

The door slammed behind him. In the electric silence, I watched Mrs. Handy lean her hands on the desk and lower herself slowly back into her chair.

"Shiiiit," muttered one of the black girls at our table, drawing the word out like a growl.

"You know what I'm saying?" I recognized Sherri Thomas's raspy voice. She was one of the four black kids in our Advanced Placement track. If she was mad enough to speak up, I knew the situation was bad. I bent my head over my book, the next best thing to disappearing.

But Sylvie hadn't noticed. "Whoa!" she said, too loudly. "That was a trip!"

I didn't have to look to know how the black girls were glaring at her.

That wasn't how I wanted to think about Sylvie. I didn't want to imagine how the black girls saw her, with her Grateful Dead jeans jacket and bouncy walk, or wonder if she got hassled in the halls like the rest of us did. I wanted to think about her the way she was when we were alone, and together, and no one else was there—at Brewster Park, for instance, sitting on the old stone bridge in the slanted October sun:

Sylvie, sleepily: "We're *alive,* man. You know? We're alive right now."

Me: "I guess."

But I did know; I knew exactly. I could feel every separate inch of my skin thrilling to the heat, a million breathing cells, and Sylvie beside me, her body a mirror of my own. We *were* alive. We were alive and I wasn't afraid.

—

That fall was a strange one, warm and green. The days had shortened but everything else stayed the same: The afternoons were hot; the leaves didn't turn. It was as though the normal consequences of things had been suspended.

I knew it couldn't last. Winter would come; I would have to make a choice: apply to college or commit to driving cross-country with Sylvie. But whenever I tried to think about any of that, a weird arbitrariness would come over me, a dizzy, free-falling sense that it didn't really matter what I did.

Walking in front of the bus, for instance: It was nothing I wanted to do and yet when I saw the bus coming a voice in my head would say, *Go ahead, step off the curb,* and I'd think, Why not? I wasn't suicidal, it was just that "Do it" and "Don't do it" suddenly had the same weight, which was no weight at all, and for a few seconds, watching the bus speed toward me, my heart would fly up like a gull, just spring up out of the way and wait. Then the bus would pull over, the door would hiss open, and I would step on. And everything on the bus would be normal—the same people, the same plastic seats, the same view of the park passing by the metal-edged windows—and I would sit down, a little breathless, like someone who had nearly fallen.

—

There was one last warm day in November. Sylvie and I spent it at Brewster Park, smoking pot and watching the clouds shape-change across the sky. Afterward, she walked me downtown to the restaurant where I was supposed to meet my father for our monthly dinner. Darkness had fallen and a crazy wind was snatching little clumps of twigs off the trees and flinging them down around us; I remember feeling happy.

The dinner was what it always was, awkward and long, but I was used to that. When my father dropped me off at home afterward, I found my mother waiting for me at the kitchen table. I was used to that, too; only this time, instead of grilling me about my dad, she began to talk about college. Somehow she'd overheard enough of my conversations with Sylvie to understand that college might not be in my plans.

I leaned against the kitchen counter, arms crossed, while I waited for her to finish. It was the usual stuff: money and jobs and social status; opportunities not to be missed. I didn't really care what she thought, so what harm could it do to stand there? But she was drunk and struggling to keep her words from slurring, and I couldn't help noticing that she looked precisely like the foolish, incompetent person my father believed her to be.

"You simply *have* to go to a good school," she said, waving her hand in the air, open-fingered, like an old-fashioned movie star. "It's just a basic requirement." With her pinkie still extended, she took a little sip of her drink, and I saw that she was entertaining some flattering idea about herself. "A basic requirement, that is," she said again, setting her drink carefully on the table, "if you want to *be* anyone."

The banked misery in my chest took fire. "Anyone like *you*?" I said.

Her startled eyes locked on mine. "What?"

"*'What?'* Jesus! You can't even hold a normal conversation."

"Casey!" she cried. "I'm trying to help! I'm trying to keep you from making a terrible, terrible mistake!"

"Yeah, well, thanks, but I don't really think you're qualified to be giving advice."

She blinked rapidly. "What?"

I should have stopped then—the whole thing was pointless anyway—but I was itching to hurt her. "Look at yourself, Mom," I said. "You're a drunk, okay? A goddamn drunk who never leaves the house."

I stomped up the stairs and left her there. Crying, probably.

So let her. I hated her for being hated, and my father for hating her, and myself, too, for being a part of it.

—

That night, the weather turned bitter and the leaves all fell at once, like stunned birds. I walked to school with Sylvie through the frozen piles the next morning, dark with foreboding. It should have been a good day. Our class was going to a college fair at a high school in one of the surrounding suburbs and Sylvie and I were planning to slip away once we got there—smoke a jay, see if we could find a coffee shop to hang out in. Only now, for some reason, I wasn't looking forward to it.

"Fuckin' college," Sylvie said, dragging her feet in the leaves. She stopped and looked at me, her face pale and exposed. "You know?"

"Yeah, I guess," I said, averting my eyes. I couldn't understand why she got so petulant and weird whenever the subject of college came up. Why did she care? She wasn't even planning to go. Besides, we were late and I had to sell a couple of joints to a girl from Social Studies before we got on the bus. "Look," I said, "I gotta hook up with that girl. Want to come?"

She sighed. "It's fuckin' cold, you know?"

"Yeah, okay," I said, turning away. I wasn't going to beg her.

Of course the girl wasn't there. I walked back and forth in front of the swings, fingering the pink plastic Tampax case I kept my joints in. I was seriously cold—the boys at the side door had pulled off my down vest a few weeks before, so all I had on was my hoodie. Also, I was worried that the bus would leave without me. By the time I saw the Social Studies girl coming up the sandy bank by the sidewalk, I was so anxious to get going, I barely even glanced around. We were still making the exchange when I noticed the group of black girls coming across the park.

There were four or five of them, walking toward us in a ragged line. Not the clean, well-dressed girls who went to class with us but the kind who hung out in the bathrooms all day, harassing anyone stupid enough to venture in.

"Hey!" called the tall one in front, her chin up like a hunting dog's. "Hey! What you got?"

The Social Studies girl whirled around, her eyes wide. "Oh shit!" she yelped.

"*Shhh,*" I said, shoving the Tampax case in my pocket. "And for chrissake, don't run," I added, like she was the problem. She gave me a resentful look but she fell into step beside me and we speed-walked down the little slope that led to the street.

"You better stop," the tall girl was saying. "You better stop 'fore I bust you skinny ass!"

It was the same old nightmare: the rabbit kick of my heart, the slipstream of faces turning to look, to watch us humiliate ourselves by running away. But I couldn't bring myself to stop, to face whatever it was they might do to us.

Maybe they didn't really want to catch up, I don't know, but somehow we reached the bus ahead of them. The Social Studies girl split off and headed for the main entrance and I leapt through the bus's folding doors and up the two short stairs. The tall girl, the one who'd started the whole thing, put her head inside the door and raised her foot like she was going to come in after me, but then she just laughed and turned away. She'd had her fun.

I stood there for a moment, holding on to one of the poles by the driver's seat. No one looked up; no one seemed to have noticed anything. The trouble I'd just been in, if you could call it that, was purely my own.

Sylvie was sitting with Robert near the back. She was smiling now, warmed up and awake. James, I remembered, was home with a cold.

"Yo," she said, as I ducked into the seat behind them, "you got the Tampax?"

I never gave her my pot—I never gave anyone my pot—but I took out the Tampax case and tossed it to her. She caught it and turned back to Robert—no "thanks," no nothing. I sat down and put my frozen hands under my armpits. I didn't care; I didn't want to talk to her anyway. A familiar darkness was falling over my mind; all I wanted was to give in to it.

"Someone sitting here?" It was Sherri Thomas.

I looked up into her curved, mahogany face and shook

my head. I didn't have the nerve to say no to her. Plus I knew she wasn't likely to talk to me; she would have sat somewhere else if she could have. I moved over and leaned my head against the cold window. We were already on the highway when I heard her say my name. I lifted my head.

"Where you applying? To college, I mean."

"Oh. Um, I don't know."

"Oh." She turned away and stared off at the front of the bus.

I hadn't thought about Sherri in connection with college. I hadn't thought about her at all, really. She was just Sherri: quick, short, good at math. I stole a glance at her. She still looked exactly as she had in ninth grade—slim and almost completely flat—and she still wore her hair the way she always had, pulled back in swirly pigtails with those colorful plastic-ball elastics. It wasn't the style; most of the black girls did their hair in sophisticated-looking curls and updos, but Sherri's reputation didn't seem to have suffered for it. She was the manager of the girls' basketball team, and popular outside the AP track, where it mattered. *She* didn't have to worry about getting jumped; she could walk anywhere, talk to anyone she wanted.

It seemed like I ought to say something, so I said, "What about you?"

She shrugged without meeting my eyes, and I remembered suddenly that she'd been there for that incident in homeroom. She probably couldn't stand me. I turned and gazed out at the gray posts of the guardrail whipping past.

"I bet you could be whatever you want, huh?" she said softly.

There was something in her voice—a cracking or breaking, the raw sound of emotion. Instinctively, I turned on her a face of bright dismissal. "Me?" I said. "No way."

Her eyes clung to mine for a second, searching; then she looked away.

I had been thinking of myself—whether she disliked me; when I could get away with leaning my head back against the window—but the look in her eyes stung me. Staring at her shut face, I wondered: What if she didn't get in anywhere? Or couldn't afford to go? Because she was poor, of course, I knew that; when she walked to school in the morning, she came over the hill with all the other black kids. I just hadn't really thought about that before, about what it might mean.

"No," I said. "Listen, I'm in the same boat as you."

She looked at me. "For real?"

"Of course," I said. "Totally. I have no clue what schools I'll get into. Or, you know, if I'll even get in."

"Huh," she said.

I took in a strained breath, like I was struggling to make headway against a stiff wind. "There's lots of schools," I went on. "I mean, we're bound to get in *somewhere,* you know?"

"I guess," she said doubtfully, though her expression softened.

"I mean even if we're rejected everywhere else, there's

always Quinnipiac. There's no *way* we wouldn't get into Quinnipiac."

She smiled a little. "I know, right?"

I leaned back, relieved. It made me feel better to have her agree. "Whitney's older brother got in there and he's a total waste case," I said. "Remember him? Whitney Peabody?"

She snorted. "Yeah. 'Last Name Last Name.'"

That had been my joke; it had never occurred to me that she might have overheard it. A bubble of elation swelled in my throat. I'd always thought of Sherri as someone who couldn't stand us, who only put up with us because she was in our class and had no choice. But she'd heard that joke; she'd thought it was funny.

"So," she said, her voice lighter, "if you could get into any college you wanted, where would you go?"

"Casey's not going to college, man." It was Sylvie. She had turned around in her seat and was grinning back at us. "Casey's going to the college of life. Right, Case? That's the real deal. The college of fuckin' *life*."

Sherri stared, her bottom lip hanging down in disgust. I looked at Sylvie, at the frayed jeans jacket and unbrushed hair, the happy, self-satisfied smile, and a steely anger flashed in me.

"No," I said sharply, "I'm going to college."

It wasn't a decision, really—I didn't even know if I meant it—but I met Sylvie's eyes with a flat stare of defiance. A small shock seemed to register in her pupils, then a hardness came over them, and she turned back around in her seat. I didn't care. I was suddenly sick of her deciding everything.

—

She and Robert must have taken off as soon as we stopped because I never even saw them come into the auditorium. When we filed back onto the bus a few hours later, they were already there, sitting against the window in the very last seat, her blond head resting against his dark one. They looked lit up, set apart, like they were famous or beautiful, something the rest of us weren't.

I sat in front with one of the Brainiac girls; I knew better than to go back there.

I was sorry then, of course. I was sorry all weekend, watching TV alone in the den. No one called, not even James. Still, by Sunday night I had formed a wild hope that I could patch things up with Sylvie. Maybe she'd seek me out at school, act as though nothing had happened. And why not? It wasn't as though we'd had an actual fight. But when she came into homeroom the next day, she gave her late pass to Mrs. Handy and sat down at one of the other tables without even glancing at me. Then the full weight of what I'd lost came home to me, and I hunched over the blurry type of my book, stricken.

"I'm just lookin'!" It was a boy at Sylvie's table, the only boy; he was holding one of the pattern books up in the air.

The girl next to him giggled and lunged for it. "Damn, girl!" he said, jerking his arm away. "Can't I just look?"

The girl sat back down, smiling. "Daryl gonna do him some sewing," she said to her girlfriend. "You gonna make me a dress, Daryl?"

I watched them, just to distract myself from the childish knot in my throat. Daryl's close-cropped hair had a linty, unwashed look, but the girls were both dressed with the usual unerring neatness: pressed shirts, matching shoes, the big, fake-gold alphabet jewelry that was in style. Sylvie sat across from them, staring at a spot on the table, her eyes puffy and red. *Still getting stoned on my pot*, I thought bitterly.

"Now that's some nice hair," Daryl was saying, peering into the pattern book. "All smooth and shit? Damn."

"Lemme see," the girl said.

"That's what I'm talking about," Daryl said, holding up the book. He pointed at the picture, a blond woman with a French twist. "*Nice* hair," he said.

I glanced at the black girl's hair. It had been straightened across her scalp and curled in large, neat rolls.

"Like her all's hair," Daryl said, pointing at Sylvie. "Smooth, you know? Not all black and nappy and shit."

The girl's face froze. I saw Sylvie drag her red eyes from the boy to the girl and then back again, slowly registering. She was going to get herself into trouble, I could see it. Watching her beautiful, unreachable face, I felt an ugly thrill of excitement.

She pushed her hair back and turned to the boy. "Nah, man," she said, smiling, "her hair's cool. It's all cool, man."

—

They caught up with Sylvie at the end of first period, the girl from homeroom, her sister, and three others. Robert stopped me in the hall to tell me as I was leaving to buy my weekly supply. They'd been unusually rough, he said—scratched her face up, got her down against the wall, where they could kick her.

"I think she might have broken a couple of ribs," he said. He leaned in and dropped his voice a little. "And she had, you know, an *accident*."

I looked back at him blankly.

"You know, lost control of her bladder?" He said it like a doctor might have, like my father. There was no trace now of whatever had lit his face on the bus.

I backed away, sickened. "Okay," I said, "thanks." Then I turned around and started walking blindly for the side door.

I don't know what I was thinking; I guess I wasn't thinking. I was just trying to get out of there, get someplace I could clear my head. I was already halfway down the stairs before I noticed the boys standing in the doorway.

"That's right, come on down, baby," the big one said, grabbing at his crotch. "I got something for you right here." The others burst out laughing and reached over to slap him five.

I froze, midstep. And then, as I looked down at their gleeful faces, something snapped inside me. Who were they to push us around? To tell us what we could or couldn't say or wear or do, rough us up just because they felt like it? What gave them the right? Rage surged up in me, hot and true, and suddenly I felt strong; I felt more powerful than any of them.

I ran down the last flight of steps and went right at them. I saw their hands come out, grabbing, but I didn't care. I stopped in front of the big one and jabbed my finger in his chest. "It's just because I'm white!" I yelled. "That's the only fuckin' reason: 'cause I'm white!"

Like magic, the hands fell away. Their faces had gone slack. "That's the only reason," I shouted. "And you know what?" They stared back at me, mute as cows, and I felt a vicious joy soar inside me. "I'm fuckin' *sick* of it!"

Then I stepped right past them into the safe, bright air. After a moment I could hear them yelling things of their own, but I didn't bother to listen. I suddenly understood they weren't going to leave that doorway.

In the park, I stopped and sat down on one of the swings to catch my breath. I shoved my foot into the newly dead leaves and pushed the swing in a crooked arc. I'd finally done it: I'd won. I thought that to myself a few times as I swung back and forth, the leftover adrenaline still sparking in my limbs: *I won, I won.* I was waiting to feel proud, or whatever it was you got to feel when you weren't the loser, when you were the one who walked away with your head held high.

But I didn't feel proud. I didn't even feel good. What I felt like was a cheat.

I put my other foot down and stopped the swing. Why should *I* feel bad? They were the ones who'd been picking on me. All I'd done was to tell the truth. I thought this and then, like an answer, I saw the face of the basketball player in homeroom that morning when Mrs. Handy let Sylvie and me get away with being late.

Like an Escher drawing, the world flipped into its opposite. My cheeks burned.

It wasn't true what I'd shouted at those boys. Or it was, but it was only a part of the truth, and saying it like that made it a kind of lie. It was one more wrong in a mess of wrongs that had started before we were even born—a mess that was ours now, whether we wanted it or not.

I leaned my hot face against the swing chain. Suddenly, I knew that I would go to college; maybe I'd always known. I would go to college and afterward I would move someplace where no one even thought about kicking my ass, much less tried it. That was the path my parents had laid out for me and I would take it; I would leave those black kids behind. What Sherri was afraid of, what I'd tried to talk her out of, was real.

Already, I could sense the relief it would be to give in, go along. But I sat there for a while before I started for home, feeling the cold weight of the air pressing down on me and Sylvie and Sherri and those boys and every other thing in that broken, screwed-up place, like a punishment we should have known was coming.

SIEGE

Randall wasn't their father, or even their stepfather, and they couldn't have given a rat's ass about his problems with the police or anyone else, but it just so happened that Danny and Amber were both at the house when the SUV from the sheriff's office drove up, and by the time they realized there was going to be trouble, Randall had already bolted the door and taken out a gun.

Now they were stuck, sitting on the floor with their backs against the half circle of sagging, dog-stinking furniture: Danny, Amber, Jason, the pit bulls Axl and Rose, and over by the window with the gun and a bottle of Jack Daniel's, Randall, their mother's last boyfriend.

Family friggin' reunion, thought Amber. The loudspeaker and the phone had both gone quiet. So Jason could negotiate, she guessed. But Jason wasn't negotiating; he was staring at her. In one of his moods—she could tell from the way his jaw was shoved forward. He'd been like that ever since he got out of the sheriff's SUV and barged across the lawn to the door, something she was pretty sure he wasn't supposed to do, given the way the cop with the speaker thing had yelled at him. They'd brought him in so he could convince Randall to let them go—that's what Jason said, anyway—but it was hard to see how that was going to happen, now that he was trapped, too.

"We got plans and we got the ordnance to carry 'em out," Randall said for what must have been the tenth time. "I got my militia buddies out there right now."

"Militia my ass," Danny said, but not too loud. They all knew how Randall could get when he drank, and the JD was already half gone. Also there was the gun to consider—not the sort of rifle a hunter would carry but something you'd see in a war movie, with the jutting handle of a machine gun and one of those things to look through on top. How an unemployed guy with a record had gotten hold of that was something Amber couldn't understand. Maybe there *was* some sort of group.

She ran her hand along the spiky fur between Axl's eyes. The dog swallowed happily and pressed his jawbone a little deeper into her leg. She could feel Jason looking at her, but she didn't care; she wasn't going to let him get to her. She had changed in the year she'd been away: turned sixteen, grown into a C-cup, gotten a new look. In her high school in Springfield, she actually had friends; she even had a boyfriend. She was in a band, too, a grunge-type thing that her boyfriend, Julian, and his buddies had started, as backup singer—or she would be, when Julian got the songs figured out.

Julian. She loved his name. It seemed to embody every-thing unique about him—his shoulder-length hair; his clear, hazel eyes; the way his long, artistic fingers strummed the guitar; even the huge, high space of his mother's kitchen, which she'd seen once when his parents were away. Like a church, it had looked, with the sun shining down through a big window cut into the ceiling.

Randall fixed them with his watery blue eyes. "I got twenty, thirty guys out there," he said, "just waitin' on night-fall." When no one answered, he took a sloppy gulp of the JD and turned back to the window.

"So what're we gonna do?" Danny said to Jason in a low voice.

But Jason was still staring at Amber. "Your hair looks like shit," he said. "What are you supposed to be, some kind of punk?"

"Shut up, Jason," Amber said.

"*Shut up, Jason,*" he mimicked.

He was as small as ever, at least five inches shorter than Danny, and thin, too. He didn't have the big Plaski bones like she and Danny did, or the wide, shield-shaped face. He was more like a weasel or a ferret, narrow and quick.

Danny swiped at the sweat on his forehead. "Jason, you gonna negotiate or what?" he said.

"Randall," Jason called over his shoulder, "you gonna let us go or what?"

"What're you, nuts? You're my friggin' hostages."

"There's your answer." Jason shrugged. He narrowed his eyes on Amber. "Is that purple in your hair? That sure as hell better not be purple."

"What's it to you?" Amber said.

"Purple's a dyke color. What are you now, a dyke?"

Amber concentrated on her hand, smoothing down the dog's fur. In the old days, she would have tried to defend herself and he would have taken everything she said and twisted it into something else he could rag on her for. And then of course she would have cried; she was always crying back then. *Amboo-hoo* they had called her. Now she knew better.

"Gotta have hostages," Randall said.

He had the gun jammed up against his cheek so he could look through the sight thing on top. Concentrating—Amber could tell by the dorky way his tongue was sticking out. Randall always had been sort of a dork, but he wasn't so bad, really. He'd had a couple feel-her-ups with her but it wasn't anything new, one of her mother's other boyfriends had been there before and a childhood friend of Danny's, too. She had just held her breath and thought about something else until she saw a chance to get away. And Randall did work sometimes. He'd help out with a roofing job once in a while, and one time he'd worked for a landscaper for a couple of weeks. Mostly, though, he just hung around the house drinking and coming up with ways to get rich. He would sit at the kitchen table and write his plans on paper plates. Golf balls was one idea—collecting them outside of golf courses and then reselling them. Japanese car parts was another. And there was some long, involved scheme about playing black-jack at the Indian casino in Connecticut, although Amber had never understood how it was supposed to work. He'd get all jazzed and go on and on about whatever it was, but after a couple of days he'd stop talking about it and if you ever brought it up, he'd snort and say, "What're you, nuts?"

The trouble came when he got skunked. Usually he just drank beer or, when her mother was still alive, the vodka and orange juice she'd always favored. But every so often, a dark, suspicious mood would come over him and he'd start in with the whiskey. It was on one of those nights that he'd broken Danny's jaw—just suddenly hauled his arm back and started slugging him in the face, and then, when their mother tried to stop him, thrown her against the wall so hard she blacked out. Jason called the cops on him that time and there was a big hoopla with a restraining order and court hearings and all that, although nothing ever came of it. Their mother stopped answering the legal advocate's calls, and a few weeks later Randall was back at the house like always. By the end, when the drinking was finally killing her, he'd pretty much kept to himself anyway.

Their mother had been nice in those last few months. Weird to look at—her arms and legs were like sticks and her belly was as big as a pregnant woman's—but sweet in a way she'd never been before. One night near the end she had sat with Amber on the porch and watched the fireflies flashing above the overgrown scruff of the backyard. It was the kind of thing she never did, and looking at her, sitting there so quietly, Amber had suddenly felt afraid.

"They're cool, you know? The fireflies?" Amber blurted. "And you can't never tell where they're gonna be. First over here, then over there—" She stopped herself; she was running at the mouth.

"That's true," her mother said in a faraway voice.

Then there was a noise behind them and Amber turned around to see Danny standing in the doorway. Only he didn't make fun of her or tell them to shut up or anything, and the three of them just stayed there, not speaking, while the fireflies flashed on and off in the dark.

A few days later her mother started pissing blue and Randall took her to the hospital. The funeral was a cheap, quick affair with a plain wooden coffin that looked too short to even fit her and a couple bunches of frayed carnations. Not that they had any right to complain. The church had paid for it, and who was there to impress anyway? It was just the four of them and Mrs. White, their nosy neighbor from up the road. Randall said he'd take care of the headstone later, but somehow it never happened and they all went their separate ways—Jason to college, Danny to his girlfriend's, Amber to the foster home in Springfield. They wouldn't have been back either, if Amber hadn't asked Danny to drive her out to pick up her summer clothes. It was Randall's house now; at least he was the one who lived in it.

Randall put down the gun and rubbed the sweat away from his eyes. "Whew! Wish I had one of my guys here right now to spell me."

"It's not like an attack or anything," Danny said wearily. "They just want to talk to you."

"You bet your ass it's an attack," Randall said, "They're trying to take the house." He picked up the bottle of JD and waved it at them. "They'll take it all, we don't fight back—our houses, our guns, everything. If you numbnuts knew what's what, you'd be fightin' with me." He took a swig and put the bottle down on its edge. It wobbled and fell over. "Whoopsie," he said, grabbing for it.

"Great," Danny muttered.

Amber giggled.

"What's so funny, lesbo?" Jason said.

She made herself look him straight in the eye. "I've got a boyfriend, asshole."

"A boyfriend! Wow! Ambo's got a boyfriend."

Randall stopped trying to get the bottle to stand up and took another drink. "You think the Zionist government ain't gonna take away *your* rights? Man! I got news for you."

"So this *boyfriend,*" Jason said to Amber. "How much does he pay you?"

Danny barked out a laugh. "Harsh!" he said, reaching over to slap Jason five.

Amber felt herself go red. She had thought, somehow, that Danny would stick up for her.

"No, wait," Jason said, "let me guess. Ten bucks? No, too much. Five? Is it five?"

She bent her face over the dog. Why did she always do that—blab out the very thing they could attack her with? That was her problem: She couldn't keep her mouth closed. "Would you shut up already?" Julian had said to her last week in front of the band. And she did it, too—shut up and sat down while they talked the song over without her. They'd made it up afterward, though. In the doorway of the Jehovah's Witness church, with her back against the ridges of the paneled wooden door. For the hundredth time, she summoned the feeling of his fingers inching up her shirt, the sweet-sharp pain of him pushing into her.

She didn't see Jason coming at her until his face was nearly touching hers. "Boo!" he spat. Her body jerked like she'd been shocked.

Jason hooted. "Look how nervous! Huh? You see that?" he said, grinning at Danny.

Tears stung Amber's eyes, she couldn't help it. She ducked her head so they wouldn't see.

"Lay off her, will ya?" Randall said. Amber heard the clunk of the bottle bumping into something, the gun maybe. "You're a couple of numbnuts, you know that? Couple of friggin' numbnuts who don't know what's what."

For a few minutes, no one said anything.

"Jason," Danny said finally, "I thought you were supposed to negotiate."

"I already did," Jason said. "You heard me." He turned back to Amber. "What are you so nervous about? Huh?"

She glanced up just in time to see him lunge at her.

"Boo!" he shouted in her face. Behind his head, the brass floor lamp jerked and swayed.

Amber blinked. Now the lamp was hanging sideways at a crazy angle, tipped but not yet falling, like a person trying to right herself. Suddenly, it rocked forward and plunged out of sight with a crash.

A shot split the air. The dogs leapt to their feet, barking furiously.

"Jesus Christ, Randall!" Danny shouted. "You trying to get us killed?"

Randall looked back at them, wide-eyed. "Fuckers are closing in!"

"It was just the lamp!" Amber shouted. "Jason kicked the lamp!" But no one heard her. Her brothers were both swearing; the dogs were scrambling from room to room, barking at the windows.

"Shut those dogs up," Randall said. Then, when none of them moved, "Shut the fuckin' dogs up!"

Danny started crawling after them. "Axl! Rose! Get over here." He made a grab for Rose's leg and missed.

"Jason, go tell me their positions," Randall said.

Jason stared at him. "What're you, nuts?"

"Gotta know their positions," Randall muttered, edging toward the window. "Do you see 'em?" He turned back to look at the three of them, his face dark and featureless against the light. "Danny," he said. "Go to the kitchen and—"

He was already falling by the time they heard the shot. Something wet sprayed Amber's face and arms.

Later, when she thought back on it, Amber would remember the next few minutes unfolding in silence, like a movie on mute. The dogs were going crazy and Danny was swearing and behind the couch Jason was saying *JesusChristJesusChrist,* but she couldn't hear any of that; she was staring at Randall. He lay on his face on the floor, an arm and a leg folded under him—crumpled, like something emptied out and tossed on the side of the road.

Amber ran a sleeve across her wet face and stood up.

"Get *down*!" Danny hissed.

But she had to go to Randall; she had to put her hands on him. Not to see if he was dead—that thought hadn't come to her yet—but to keep him from being all by himself like that. She crouched down beside him and laid her hand between his shoulder blades. His T-shirt was warm beneath her palm, like anyone's.

"Randall," she said, patting him there, "Randall." Then, because she didn't know what else to do, she put her hands on either side of the strange, neat hole in the back of his head and gently turned his face up.

A bloody crater, welling.

"Oh, Christ!" Danny gasped.

She jerked her hands away and bent over herself, sucking

at the air. She could hear one of her brothers—Jason?—throwing up. She forced back an answering surge of bile.

"IT'S OKAY," the loudspeaker announced. "IT'S ALL OVER."

Another breath and another. She was trying to make her stomach quiet so she could get up and tell them to hurry and get the ambulance, get the medics or whatever they called those people—hurry up before it was too late. A train of thought like in a dream, the things she should be doing sliding like water through her hands.

By the time she was able to push herself up, she understood enough not to call out to them. She took the few short steps to the shattered window and looked out. The blunt metal noses of the SUVs stared back at her, shiny and whole.

"IT'S OKAY, AMBER," the loudspeaker said. "IT'S ALL OVER."

She spotted the curled black cord of the loudspeaker coming out of one of the cars' windows.

"JUST SECURE THE DOGS, OKAY? AND THEN YOU AND YOUR BROTHERS CAN COME ON OUT."

You and your brothers. Not Randall. Randall was dead.

She turned around to see what her brothers were going to do, but they seemed oddly unconcerned. Jason was still standing behind the couch, wiping the puke off his mouth with the hem of his shirt; Danny was chasing after Axl. He glanced back at her from the other side of the room, his face white and strangely askew. "I guess we should get some rope?" he said.

To secure the dogs he meant.

"IT'S ALL RIGHT," the loudspeaker said, "YOU CAN COME ON OUT NOW." The tone was one of practiced, professional kindness—the sort of tone her teachers used, and the social workers at the state children's agency. Smooth, friendly sounding voices that hid the hard shove of command underneath: *Sign here. That's enough, now. Let's not make this any harder than it has to be.* You did it, of course. Over the sickened, hangdog feeling of not wanting to, you did what they said.

But that was Randall lying there.

"Amber, give me a hand, will ya?" Danny said. He was trying to get Rose now, lunging at her collar as she streaked past.

Amber didn't answer. Something was sharpening in her chest, furious and cold.

"IT'S ALL RIGHT NOW," the loudspeaker said again. "IT'S ALL OVER."

No, she thought; *not over.* Randall's gun lay under the window in a scatter of glass. She bent over and picked it up. It was heavier than she'd thought it would be, and there were two parts that stuck out from the barrel, so at first she grabbed the wrong one, the one without the trigger. But it didn't matter, she was still moving, still gliding on the sharp, clean blade of her rage.

"JUST LEASH THE DOGS," the loudspeaker was saying. "OR YOU COULD JUST SECURE THEM IN A ROOM. WHATEVER'S EASIEST."

"Amber," Danny called from the kitchen, "you gonna give me a hand or what?"

She didn't bother to crouch down like Randall had; she just pressed the butt of the gun against her shoulder like she'd seen him do and felt for the trigger. There it was, curved and smooth; it hooked around her finger like it had been waiting. She pulled it and the gun kicked back hard against her. Through the concussion in her ears, she heard the dogs burst into another frenzy of barking. She lowered the gun and looked. One of the SUV's headlights was gone.

"Amber!" Danny shouted. "What the fuck!"

But she was feeling all right now, she was actually feeling sort of good. She raised the gun again. This time she put her eye to the looking thing on top: four thin black lines in a cross. She moved a little so that the other headlight floated into the middle. Bam! Gone. Elation opened in her chest like wings.

"HOLD YOUR FIRE," the loudspeaker blared, "HOLD YOUR FIRE!" There was a flurry of activity behind the line of vehicles; she could see boots scurrying in the narrow gap just above the pavement.

"Amber! Put that down!" Danny cried, his eyes gone dark.

"It's okay," she shouted to him over the noise of the dogs. They were going nuts now—howling, leaping at the windows, flecks of saliva flying off their mouths. "Axl!" she called. "Rose! Get over here!" They stopped barking and came across the room to her, wagging their butts. This did not surprise her—it seemed of a piece with the rest of it: with hitting the headlights, with the strange, clear power that was guiding her. She put her free hand on Axl's back and pressed. "Down," she said. Whining, he buckled his legs and settled tensely on top of them. Then she put her hand on Rose and pushed her down, too.

When she looked up again, Danny was standing right in front of her. Her heart skidded in her chest.

"Give it to me," he said. *"Now."*

She didn't mean to turn the gun on him; it was just a reflex, like raising her arm to ward off a blow.

Immediately he stumbled backward, his hands flying up. "Okay! Okay! Jesus!"

For a long moment, they faced each other, not moving. There was a noise in her head, a roaring, but under that nothing, blankness.

Danny let his weight shift forward. "Amb—"

"Get back!" she gasped.

They stared at each other.

"Sit!" she said. "Sit down!"

Amazingly, he did what she said; he backed up and lowered himself onto the couch.

"No way," Jason said. He started walking out from behind the couch. "No way is she doing this."

"Take it easy," Danny said, holding up his hand. "Don't—don't—"

"No," Jason said, knocking Danny's arm aside. "No, you know what? *I'm* gonna handle this. Amber! Drop the fucking gun!"

"Jason!" Danny hissed.

Jason whirled around to face him. "Fuck off and let me handle this, okay? Just fucking fuck off for once in your life."

"AMBER, THIS IS DEPUTY O'NEILL," the loudspeaker said. "I CAN SEE YOU'RE UPSET. I'D LIKE TO HEAR ABOUT WHY, OKAY? SO LISTEN, I'M GOING TO GIVE YOU A CALL ON THE PHONE NOW. SO WE CAN TALK, OKAY?"

"Listen, you douche bag," Jason said, "you put that gun down *now*. Or no—you know what?" He took a step forward. "I'll get it myself."

"Sit!" Amber squeaked. And then, like an idiot, "Or else."

His eyes lit. "Or else what? Huh? What're you gonna do, shoot me?"

She raised the gun shakily to the level of his chest. Danny reached out and grabbed Jason's arm. "Sit the fuck down," he said.

"Fuck off," Jason said, jerking away, but he let himself fall with exaggerated slowness onto the couch.

Their eyes, looking back at her, were hard and merciless.

"ALL YOU HAVE TO DO IS PICK UP THE PHONE. YOU CAN STAY RIGHT WHERE YOU

ARE AND WE'LL STAY RIGHT WHERE WE ARE AND WE'LL JUST TALK ON THE PHONE. OKAY? HERE GOES."

The phone on the little white table began to ring. It had been her mother's table, the one next to her bed. The memory of its smell came to her: baby powder and vodka and the waxy perfume of the ancient pink lipstick that used to roll around in the back; the queer, mixed-up odor of comfort and disease.

But it was too late for that now.

A darkness closed over her brain and she felt her knees give way, and then the hard surface of the wall against her back as she slid down toward the floor.

—

They had taken the back roads that morning, she and Danny, driving out of the city in a lazy-morning hush, past the strip malls and the trailer park to the place where the buildings thinned out and the road began to climb and curve. The lots were larger here, the houses separated by stray, forgotten patches of woods, the occasional field with its tumbledown wall of stones. The air flowing past the car window was cool enough, but Amber could feel the heat that was coming. Over ninety, it was supposed to be, a record for April. There was an odd sensation of rooflessness, even in the woods; the trees hadn't leafed out yet and the shade they cast was thin and veiny.

Amber had told her Springfield friends she didn't want to go home, but secretly she'd been excited. She had washed her new pink leopard skirt the night before, waking up early to blow-dry the damp spots, and she'd taken extra care with the hair gel and black eyeliner she'd started using. She wanted Danny and Randall to see her as she was now—not just her changed body but the boots and the spiky hair and the rest of it. A look that would be strange to them, that would mark her as belonging someplace else now, someplace they didn't understand and might not be welcome.

That was what she had thought, anyway, although Danny barely seemed to notice. "Hey," he'd said when she came out to get in the car—friendly enough, but after a "how ya doin'?" and a few other standard questions, they had run out of things to say. He was silent, driving with one hand, slapping his leg along to the heavy metal on the radio.

The house had come up suddenly, as it always did, from behind the clump of evergreens by the road. It had been her grandfather's, built with his own hands—or so the story went, although once their mom had admitted that the pieces had come premade in some kind of kit. Amber and her brothers had moved in with their mom after their grandfather went to jail, when Amber was seven.

The house looked smaller than she remembered, and dirtier—more gray now than white. Little trees had sprouted all over the lawn, whip-thin above the pale, knocked-down winter grass. Someone, probably Randall, had hacked back the ones against the house and now the new growth was coming straight out the top, like knots of shiny hair.

Danny drove to the end of the driveway and cut off the engine. In the quiet, they could hear the dogs barking inside the house. Amber got out of the car and smoothed down her skirt, suddenly nervous.

"Look, we can't hang out, okay?" Danny said, slamming the car door. "I gotta be back at two to take Theresa to the doctor's." Theresa was his girlfriend, the same one he'd had since high school. One of those perfect girls with layered hair and just the right amount of makeup. She'd been a majorette, back then.

"I know," Amber said.

"I'm just sayin'."

The screen door flew open and the dogs burst out, slobbering and whining, wagging their stumpy tails. They found Randall inside, sitting at the kitchen table in an undershirt, his hair sticking up every which way.

"Hey, Randall," Danny said over the noise.

"Hey," he said without looking up, like they came by every day. Or had never left.

"I just came to get my clothes," Amber said.

Randall raised his eyes and looked her up and down, and she saw herself part by part, as though she were being illuminated with a flashlight—hair, breasts, skirt, boots.

"You're lookin' growed," he said.

"Thanks." She thought he might say more but he just looked back down at the paper he was reading.

Danny was opening the fridge. "Hey, Randall, you got any food? I'm fuckin' starved."

"I dunno, take a look. Hey, you two know about this Zionist government we got going? 'Cause I got some materials right here'll blow your mind."

His newest obsession, probably. Amber looked around for a place to sit. Randall was sitting in the only free chair; the others were covered with stacks of paper, as was the table. She bent down to look at the pile nearest her: *Massacre at Ruby Ridge,* the top paper said. She picked it up and looked at the official-looking letter beneath it: *Notice of Intention to Foreclose.*

Whatever, she thought, letting the papers flap back down. Randall was still talking—the government was after his rights. Or his house? She couldn't really follow it. The spark of interest she'd felt at the idea of seeing him had fizzled. She leaned against the wall; all her energy seemed to have drained away.

"Randall, there's nothing fuckin' *in* here," Danny interrupted.

"Check down the bottom. Seriously, you gotta take a look at this. It's got facts here you ain't gonna believe."

Danny started opening the drawers at the bottom of the fridge, where the fruit and vegetables were supposed to go. "Randall, this shit is blue," he said, holding up a plastic package. "What the hell is it, anyway, bologna?"

Randall shrugged. "Could be." He shoved the paper he was reading toward Danny. "So check this out."

They seemed to have forgotten her, both of them. Jerking herself upright, Amber walked into the living room, the dogs at her heels. It was the same—dustier, the furniture more beaten down maybe, but basically the way it'd always been. On the far wall, beyond the stairs, was the curtained glass door to her mother's old bedroom. If this sight had filled her with sadness or made her eyes tear up, she could have made a story out of it to tell her friends when she got back to Springfield. But what she actually felt was nothing she could tell anyone: boredom, it seemed like, or restlessness. A buzzing, dragging dissatisfaction.

There was no place to sit down in here either; no place clean enough, anyway.

She wandered around picking things up, putting them down. A china cat, a picture of her mother from back when she was beautiful, in a blue summer dress and high heels; a little Statue of Liberty with the torch busted off. None of it seemed to have anything to do with Amber, or if it did, not in any way she wanted to think about. After a while she stopped in the middle of the room. What was she even doing there? It was embarrassing now to think back to the anticipation she'd felt, getting ready that morning.

I should just get the clothes and go, she thought. But she stood there, leaden, her limbs drained of life.

She was saved by the wheezy rumble of a vehicle coming

up the driveway—a big, dark-colored SUV with tinted windows. She had just enough time to notice the large gold star on the side of it before Randall scrambled into the room and threw himself at the front door.

—

"UH, AMBER, HI."

She was watching the floorboards jump up at her and then drop away. Up when she went forward and the sick feeling of falling took hold of her; away when her body snapped back and her spine hit the hard edge of the baseboard. A lot of time had passed—dimly, she was aware of that. The phone had rung and the loudspeaker had gone on and off, and once, from the opening and shutting of Jason's mouth, she'd realized he must be yelling at her, but these sounds were far off and broken and didn't seem quite real. She just held the gun across her like the safety bar on a carnival ride and slammed her back against the wall.

This one, though, she heard.

"OFFICER KOTLOWSKI HERE. REMEMBER ME?"

She looked up, blinking. The light was different now—reddish, slanted. Late afternoon light. Her brothers were still sprawled on the couch. Danny had his face tipped up toward the ceiling, but Jason was staring right at her. She dropped her eyes.

"WE . . . UH . . . GO WAY BACK, RIGHT?" There was a sputtering explosion as Kotlowski cleared his throat into the loudspeaker. His face came back to her: pale and round, puckered as a cauliflower. Officer Stanley Kotlowski.

"I'VE ALWAYS BEEN A FRIEND TO YOU PLASKIS."

It was what he used to say, standing wide-legged in their kitchen: *You Plaskis.* After some incident of vandalism or petty theft he would come over and stand there like that, resting his small, sunken eyes on each of them in turn. *What's wrong with you Plaskis anyway? Huh?* Shaking his head; making a show of it.

They never answered; they just sat there staring at the floor or his feet or whatever, waiting for him to be done. That was what Amber remembered about those visits: the gray Jell-O soles of his cop shoes, the curled-up edges of the fake brick linoleum. The things he was referring to, the known facts that made up the meaning of "Plaski"—that their mother was a drunk and their grandfather had killed his own wife; that everything they did was the kind of dumbass thing a Plaski would do—these were as fixed as the pale blue of their eyes or the tree-fringed patch of sky above their yard, and not worth thinking about.

"I USED TO, UH, COME CHECK ON YOU AND YOUR, UH, MOM, GODREST," the loudspeaker said.

Amber rocked back and a comforting ripple of pain radiated out from her spine. What was it he'd said to her mother, the time Randall had knocked her out? *Look at yourself.* Wasn't that it? *Look at yourself. You want to be treated nice you should fix yourself up a little.*

Amber had been the one to let him in that night, too. She'd run to the door in her panic, as though he would be the answer to everything.

"SO I'M, UH, HERE TO TALK TO YOU ABOUT STOPPING THIS NONSENSE. THESE PEOPLE ARE TRYING TO HELP YOU, OKAY? SO HOW ABOUT YOU SHOW A LITTLE RESPECT."

She felt it in her chest, a shock, as though she'd been struck. Then the surge of anger, steely and hard.

"YOU THINK YOU CAN DO THAT? SHOW A LITTLE RESPECT?"

She whipped around and fired the gun through the empty window frame—a couple of wild shots, not even aimed at anything. In the second before the dogs started barking, she heard the high-pitched hoot of Danny's laugh. She glanced over at him but his face had closed again.

"AMBER! DON'T SHOOT! WE CAN WORK THIS OUT!" It was the O'Neill guy again.

"Guess Kotlowski's out," Danny said. He made a buzzer sound, like on a game show.

Amber leaned back against the wall, a sliver of warmth cracking open in her.

Danny was right, Kotlowski *was* out, but they had found other people: nosy Mrs. White and another neighbor whose name they didn't even recognize, Sullivan or Callahan, Amber couldn't quite catch it. And then—how they came up with this one, she couldn't imagine—Mrs. Mackey, their high school guidance counselor.

"HELLOOOO! AMBER AND DANNY AND JASON! THIS IS KATHLEEN MACKEY!"

Danny lifted his head. "Who?"

"REMEMBER ME? MRS. MACKEY? FROM THE HIGH SCHOOL?"

"No way," Danny said. He stood up and glanced at Amber; then, when she made no move to stop him, walked across the room to the other window.

"WELL," the loudspeaker breathed, "HELLO, KIDS!"

"Where's she even at?" Danny said. "Behind the door?"

Cautiously, taking care to keep the gun securely under her arm, Amber got stiffly to her feet. It was cooler, standing; she could feel a breath of air coming through the broken window. "Yeah," she said after a moment. "Those are her legs, see? The bare ones. With the sneakers."

"Oh, yeah."

Behind them, Amber heard Jason get up. She turned to face him but he went straight to the window without even glancing her way.

"Well, whaddya know," he said, "Mrs. Fuckin' Douche Bag Mackey."

"I UNDERSTAND FROM THESE NICE FOLKS HERE THAT YOU'RE, UH, A LITTLE UPSET."

"I should go out there and show her my college ID," Jason said. "Give her a friggin' heart attack."

"Oh yeah," Danny said, "What was it she said? Work on a garbage truck?"

"'If I were you, young man,'" Jason said in a high, wobbly voice, "'I'd consider a career in the sanitation department.'"

What Mrs. Mackey had said to Amber was not something she could repeat: *I'd keep my legs closed, if I were you. And I'd stop wearing that slutty makeup. Do you want to end up like your mother? Does that look like fun to you?* "I thought she said mechanic," Amber muttered.

"Yeah, that was her other bright idea." A regular voice now, the kind he used with Danny. "Didn't even look at my grades. Didn't open the friggin' folder."

She glanced at him. Something about the way he was standing reminded her of how he used to look when she spotted him in the hallway in elementary school—small and thin, easy to beat on. The old, lonely pull of their siblinghood flashed up in her. "What a bitch," she said.

He shrugged. "Yeah, well."

"WE'D LIKE TO TALK ABOUT WHAT'S UPSETTING YOU," Mrs. Mackey said.

"Up yours, Mackey!" Jason yelled.

"WE'RE GOING TO GIVE YOU A CALL ON THE PHONE, OKAY? ALL YOU HAVE TO DO IS PICK UP, ALL RIGHT? JUST PICK UP THE PHONE AND WE'LL—"

"Shove it up your flabby old ass!" Jason yelled.

Amber shut her mouth to stifle a crazy bubble of laughter.

"ALL RIGHT? HERE GOES."

The phone began ringing again.

"Hey, remember that guy Eli?" Danny said.

"Eli?" Amber said. "What one was that? Oh, you mean with the glasses?"

"Yeah, Eli. You know, the dude who stuck stuff up his ass."

"No way," Amber said.

"Yes, way. Like the time he stuck the remote up his ass?" Danny waited while Mrs. Mackey said something over the loudspeaker. "Jason, you remember that, right?"

Jason raised his eyebrows. "Yeah, that was sort of a low."

The laughter came up in Amber in a rush, like vomit. But it was okay—Danny was laughing, too.

"And how about that other guy," Danny said. "What was his name? The one before Randall."

"Jimmy the Jackass!" Amber and Jason said together.

"Jimmy, yeah. Remember how he ate? Like Bugs Bunny?"

"Oh yeah! And the food got all stuck in his mustache."

"He looked like a friggin' walrus with that thing," Danny said.

Amber stifled another spurt of laughter.

"WE'D REALLY LIKE TO TALK TO YOU," Mrs. Mackey said.

"Man! That's, like, the third time she said that," Danny said. "Shoot out another light, Amber."

Even Jason laughed then, that high-pitched, girlish cackle she had forgotten.

They thought of other stuff that had happened—weird, shameful things that Amber normally didn't like to remember but which now, held up and laughed at, seemed almost something to brag about: the winter they ate everything from cans; the time their mother drove the car into the side of the garage and passed out with her head on the horn; Eli sleeping naked on the couch with Amber's teddy bear between his legs.

Amber had started shaking again, just little tremors, nothing they would notice, probably, but she leaned into the wall just in case. It was the relief, or maybe what happened to her sometimes with Julian—an excitement that was also worry that at any moment things would go bad again. Because everything was okay now; by some miracle everything was good.

It was better not to think about that, she knew; if you thought about it you might wreck it.

The sun had gone down and now a gloom was settling in beneath the still-bright sky. There was some sort of change going on outside: boots, car doors, an engine starting. When the loudspeaker came on again it was a new guy talking.

"Mackey's out," Amber said. She made the buzzer sound, like Danny.

"Wait," Danny said, "what'd he say?"

Jason shrugged. "I dunno, something about pizza."

"Pizza for us?" Amber said.

"I guess."

"Let's go for it," Danny said. "I'm starving and there sure as shit isn't anything to eat in here. What was that phone number again?"

"Beats me."

"He only said it like a million times."

"Oh and *you* remember it?" Jason flipped his hand toward the phone. "Be my guest."

"It doesn't matter," Amber said. "We can just write what we want and hold it up to the window."

"Oh yeah," Danny said. "That'd work."

Jason snorted. "Good luck finding a pen in this shithole."

Amber reached back with her free hand and fished the lipstick out of her skirt pocket. "Here," she said, tossing it to Danny. "Write it on the window. But backward," she added.

"What do you mean, backward?"

"She's right," Jason said. "It has to be backward so they can read it."

Again, the crazy, improbable feeling of hitting the target without trying; flinging things out and having them miraculously land right.

—

There were rules, it turned out. They were to stand at the window with their arms up while the officer put the food down on the lawn. Once he'd made it back to the cars, one of them could come out, but whoever it was had to stop on the porch first, still with hands in the air, and turn around slowly so they could see there was no gun.

"THIS IS VERY IMPORTANT, OKAY?" the guy on the loudspeaker said. "WE HAVE TO SEE YOU'RE UNARMED OR ELSE WE MIGHT HAVE TO TAKE STEPS TO ENSURE OUR SECURITY AND SOME- ONE COULD GET HURT."

Danny did the whole song and dance exactly as they said. It occurred to Amber, watching him from the window with the gun wedged between her feet, that he might make a run for it. But he didn't; he just stacked the three jumbo milk shakes on top of the pizza boxes and carried it all back into the living room.

"Smells good!" He grinned at Amber. "Where d'you want it?"

"I don't know. Here?" It seemed like too much trouble to clear all the crap off the kitchen chairs.

"With him?" Jason said.

How could she have forgotten about Randall? She glanced over at the huddled shape of him, sprawled behind the chair. The puddle of blood had grown unbelievably large—even the chair legs were in it now. Quickly, she went to the chair and pulled off the old, dog-hair-matted bedspread that covered it. "Here," she said, throwing the cloth over him with her free hand; then she turned away so she wouldn't have to see the edges of it soaking up the red.

They ate with their backs to him, folding the slices and jamming them into their mouths, tossing the crusts to the dogs. Not talking, not even looking at each other. The quiet made Amber nervous, so she said the first thing that came into her head: "Do you think he'll, like, haunt the house?"

"Who?" Danny said.

She jerked her head toward Randall.

Danny shrugged. "I don't know." He threw a crust and Axl snapped it out of the air. "Grandmom doesn't. It'd be her if it was anyone."

"Why Grandmom?"

Jason gave her a look.

"I mean why her and not, you know, Mom?"

"Because Mom didn't die here, stupid," Jason said.

She flushed. Of course their grandmother had died there, she knew that. And yet for some reason it had seemed to her suddenly like maybe she hadn't, like maybe in this new slapstick, shame-free version of their childhood, that might have ceased to be true. But thinking that was a mistake. A wrong move.

She shook it off. "This house sucks," she said.

"No shit," Danny said. "We should burn it down. Do the world a favor."

Jason wiped his mouth with the back of his hand. "No, what we should do is get the fuck out of here."

"Let's get the fuck out and *then* burn it down," Amber said.

Laughter, like the rush of coins down a slot machine.

There was a game they used to play in early winter when the first, brittle ice formed on the little ponds back in the woods. The goal was to slide from one side of a pond to the other without breaking through into cold water underneath. This seemed impossible—the ice would shatter if you so much as stood on it. But you could do it if you went fast enough. If you kept your feet moving, you could slide all the way across with the ice popping and seaming behind you. What you couldn't do was stop.

—

Amber had laid the gun down and was putting the pizza boxes on the floor for the dogs to lick when her foster mother's voice came over the loudspeaker. "AMBER, HONEY."

She could feel her brothers' eyes on her, the sharp silence of the room. Instinctively, she reached for the gun.

"I GOT OUT HERE SOON AS I COULD. IT JUST TOOK A WHILE, YOU KNOW, TO GET OFF WORK AND ALL.

"OH. IT'S ANGELA. I SHOULD'VE SAID THAT."

Secretly, Amber liked this voice, as she liked the other worn and comfortable things about her foster mother: the grainy shadows beneath her eyes, her heavy chest, the frank band of silver hair that ran down both sides of her part.

"I'M HERE TO SEE CAN I HELP YOU ANY. IT MUST HAVE BEEN TERRIBLE— OH!" There was an electronic squeal, then some amplified fumbling. "SORRY, HONEY. I CAN'T WORK THIS THING. THE OFFICER SAYS I COULD CALL YOU ON THE PHONE. OH, HE'S GONNA DIAL FOR ME. ALL RIGHT, THANKS."

The phone began to ring. Five rings, ten rings; it broke off.

Another squeal. "AMBER, HONEY, CAN YOU ANSWER THE PHONE?"

Amber held on to the gun and waited, a noise like the sound of the highway in her ears.

"WELL, ALL RIGHT," Angela said, finally, "I GUESS YOU'RE NOT READY." Even through the loudspeaker, Amber could hear the hurt in her voice. "I'LL COME BACK IN THE MORNING, ALL RIGHT? YOU GET SOME REST IN THERE AND I'LL TALK TO YOU TOMORROW. OKAY. I LOVE YOU. SEE YOU TOMORROW."

Amber made the buzzer sound. "Out!" she cried.

Her brothers were looking at their feet, both of them, and they didn't answer.

—

There was no more joking after that. The O'Neill guy got on the loudspeaker to tell them the rules for coming out, which were basically the same as the rules for picking up the food: no dogs, no gun, stop on the porch with hands raised. Then Jason stood up and said he was going to sleep.

Their old bedrooms were jammed with what looked like trash picks—old TVs, lawn furniture, the tented metal hands of shadeless lamps—and from the smell of it, dog shit, too. The only usable bed was the one in their mother's room, where Randall must have been sleeping. They stood outside the door, looking in at the rumpled covers. There was junk in there, too, but the bed and the area around it had been kept clear.

"You guys take it," Amber said.

"Good," Jason said. He was already walking in anyway.

Danny followed her back into the living room and stood there while she arranged a pillow at the end of the couch. "Man! Jason didn't clean up his puke."

"It's okay," Amber said.

"You sure you're okay here?" Danny said.

"Yeah, sure." She jammed the gun in the crack between the seat cushion and the couch back and lay down next to it. "Could you get the light?"

He didn't move right away, and when he did, he went slowly. The light shut off.

"Thanks," she said, but she could hear that he was still standing there. "What?"

"You're really gonna sleep with that."

"Yeah. Why?"

"I dunno. Never mind."

"What?"

"Nothing. Forget it."

She heard the creak of the loose floorboard by the bathroom and then, after a few minutes, the toilet flushing and the sound of his footsteps going into the bedroom. Then the thunk of his shoes and the bedsprings, then nothing—the soft stutter of the clock on the kitchen stove. On the floor next to her, Axl sloshed his tongue around contentedly. The room had seemed dark at first, but as she lay there the night thinned and the shapes of things began to re-form themselves: chairs, dogs, the lump that was Randall.

There's a dead person right here in this room, she thought. She waited a moment for a reaction but she felt nothing; the idea of Randall was curiously empty for her now. What came to her mind instead was something her mother used to say—used to yell—near the end.

"Beaten to death!" She would lurch around the house yelling that, her mouth sagging open in outrage: "Beaten to death! Right here in this house!" As if this was news, as if their grandmother hadn't been dead for years.

"We know, Mom," they'd mutter. Or, if she kept at it, "Mom! Shut up already!" They had said it, too, of course—to impress a friend or for the shocking thrill of it, or just as a statement of fact: beatentodeath. Now, lying in the dark,

Amber wondered what it actually meant. Hit, of course; maybe kicked. A bunch of times, it would have to have been. And her trying to get away—cowering and stumbling, crawling, even, until she came up against the final limit of the wall or the floor or the stove or whatever it was she would finally die against.

But why? Amber had never thought to ask; none of them had. They didn't need to: The answer had always been there right in front of them—in their grandmother's sagging mouth and birdlike arms, and the way she bent her head when her husband yelled at her; in what she said and how she walked and her pale, uncertain eyes. *She* was the reason, she was why.

Something floated up under the surface of Amber's mind, ghostly and sick-hued, like the ink-swamped triangle in a Magic 8 Ball. A horror. She felt it close around her in the dark.

She sat up, her body electric. But no—there were the stairs; there was the doorway leading to the kitchen. Behind her, no more than fifteen feet away, the front door. Not a trap, just the house, pretty much as she'd always known it. She lay back down, shifting a little so her thigh rested against the cool length of the gun.

She's right. Jason had said that. And, *shoot out another light*—that had been Danny. It was okay, she thought; she could sleep.

—

She woke, sweating, in bright light. There were voices outside, and the noise of heavy shoes grinding against the grit on
the pavement. How had she allowed herself to sleep so late?
Alarmed, she stood up too fast and had to steady herself on
the arm of the couch. She wiped her eyes and mouth with
her hand and twisted her skirt back around, ignoring the
pressure in her bladder. She had to find her brothers. She
fished the gun out of the crack between the cushions and,
taking care not to look over at Randall, walked toward the
kitchen. Danny and Jason were talking in there, she could
hear them. She stopped just outside the doorway to listen.

"Yeah, I know, but let me handle it, okay?" That was
Danny.

"Oh, like you've been handling it so great?" Jason said.
"You should have gotten it from her last night when you
had the chance."

"*I* should have? What, 'cause you were busy getting your
beauty rest? Give me a break. And anyway, if I'd of grabbed
it, it would have gone off, 'cause she sure as shit didn't put
the safety on. She probably doesn't even know it has one."
There was a pause. "Just—just don't jump all over her. Let
me handle it, okay?"

"Hey," Amber said, stepping over the threshold.

"Hey," Danny said. Jason just looked at her.

To buy time, she bent down to see the dogs underneath
the table. "Come here," she said, slapping her free hand
against her thigh. Axl stretched his paws out toward her and

snapped out a curled, pink-tongued yawn, but he didn't get up. "Come on, you big lazy!" she said. Then she saw: He and Rose were tied to the table legs.

"Amber," Danny said, "we gotta talk."

She straightened up slowly, her knees gone to sand.

He and Jason couldn't afford to be getting in trouble, Danny said. He had responsibilities now—Theresa was expecting; they were going to get married, probably. "And Jason here's trying to get into the Air Force, you know? He can't, you know, get himself a record or anything."

She listened to him from the side of herself, her gaze fixed on the dusty window above the sink. Pretty little Theresa in a wedding dress; pretty little Theresa with a baby.

"So—" Danny said.

"So we got to leave the house," Jason said. "Like they asked us. Without pulling any shit."

Outside, Amber could see the hard, knuckled branches of a few trees, the harsh, white sky. An emptiness. There was nothing out there, not for her anyway.

"And you can't take that gun," Jason said. "Amber, you hear me?"

She pulled her eyes away from the window. They were both watching her now, and the look in their eyes was the kind the dogs would give her if she had a steak in her hand—a look not to see her but to get around her, to spot the weakness or false move that would give them an opening.

There was a squeal from the driveway. "UM, AMBER?" A thin voice, cracked and fluty. "THIS IS JULIAN?"

"Julian?" Jason said. "What the hell kind of name is that?" Then, realizing, "Is that your *boy*friend?"

"No, that's cool," Danny said, quickly, "that's cool. I'd like to, you know, meet him."

To get her out of the house; that was all he meant. Get her out of their hair so they could go back to their lives.

"THEY SAID I SHOULD CALL YOU? SO THAT'S, UH, WHAT I'M DOING?"

Amber's heart recoiled. Why did he have to talk like that? He sounded like some kind of wuss. But there was no time to think about this because immediately the phone in the living room began to ring.

"Go ahead," Jason said, jerking his head toward the door.

"Yeah," Danny said, "go for it. We'll stay right here. Take your time. Talk things over, whatever. Whatever you want, okay?"

It was the kind of thing he used to say to her mother to get her off his back: *Sure, Mom. Sure. Whatever you want.* Amber saw her as she used to look, standing in the doorway to her bedroom, slump-shouldered and pale, her face the infuriating blank of a target.

You could be that. For your whole life, you could be that.

The ringing cut off.

"Jesus!" Jason muttered.

"Take it easy," Danny growled. "Amb," he said in a softer

voice, "it's whatever you want, okay? Whatever you want to do."

She didn't hear him. A crazy pressure was building in her chest. She looked wildly around the room, unseeing. Then she remembered the gun. It was in her hands, heavy and true.

She felt the strength flow back into her legs. She was standing between them and the living room door; she could make it if she was quick enough. "Okay, sure," she said, backing up, "whatever you want." At the doorway, she whirled around and ran—past Randall, past the white table where the phone was starting to ring again.

"Amber!" Danny said sharply.

She saw them out of the corner of her eye, running at her with their arms out, the way they would chase down one of the dogs. But it was too late, she was already at the door.

She yanked it open with her free hand and stepped out into the brightness. There was a shout from the cluster of SUVs, a uniformed arm waving high. For a split second, she felt herself against the soft air of the morning: the skin of her arms, the roots of her hair standing up as if in joy.

She raised the gun, slipped her finger through the trigger, and pulled.

FRIDAY NIGHT

Her husband called her at work every couple of hours. She would never have gotten away with it before, but now that he was in the hospital it no longer seemed to matter what she did. No one pressured her about deadlines, no one expected her at meetings. She was suddenly exempt.

The calls were all the same: medical updates, lousy food updates, nurse gossip ("gurse nossip," he called it). Ordinary calls, conducted in an ordinary tone of voice—no different, if you left aside the subject matter, from all the other daily calls they'd made during their seven years together. Now, though, when he said "I love you," she didn't want to say it back. She said it, of course. She watched the words balloon from her mouth, rubbery and hollow, and her heart shrank.

There were times—alone at night in their bed, for example—when she had the feelings she was supposed to have: grief, love, longing. But the instant she opened the door to his hospital room, all of that vanished. He looked terrible with his bald head and sunken chest, his gray, unhealthy skin. Even his beautiful eyelashes were gone,

117

even his smell, which she had loved. She had an irritable urge to rush into the room and scold: Exercise! Brush your teeth! Get a wig for chrissake! Instead, she sat down beside him and talked with him reasonably, even sweetly, until it was time to go home. It was awful. Every word, every gesture of affection seemed like a betrayal. She was acting what she used to feel.

One day, while she was idling away the time at work, she learned that a friend of theirs, a man ten years older than they, had qualified for the marathon. The news had nothing to do with her, really—he wasn't a close friend—and yet she found herself recalling it again and again over the course of the day. The thought of this man, with his firm, lean torso and clear eyes, gave her a feeling of comfort, even elation, as though she had unexpectedly had a stroke of good luck.

When she got to the hospital that afternoon, she mentioned the news to her husband.

He snorted. "So? What's so great about that?"

"What do you mean, what's so great? It's something like twenty-six miles!"

He raised the muscles where his eyebrows used to be. "Twenty-six miles? Twenty-six miles is nothing. Anyone could do that."

Anger swept up in her, sudden and fierce. "Oh, really, anyone?" she snapped. "Like you? You could just go out and run a marathon?" She froze: It was the wrong thing to say, the wrong tone.

"And why not, may I ask?" His eyes had their old, mischievous glint.

A joke. She made herself relax back in her chair. "Because," she said in a lighter tone, "you are too . . ." She searched for something innocuous. "Prone. You are just too darn prone."

"Prone?" he said. "You think I'm prone? Well, we'll see about that." He threw off the sheet and got unsteadily to his feet.

"What are you doing?"

He held his hand out to silence her. Slowly, with the exaggerated gestures of a performer, he rolled the sleeves of his hospital gown up over his skinny biceps. Then he lunged forward and bowed his arms like a bodybuilder. "Who's the man?" he said. "Who's the man?" He turned around to show his back, bouncing and flapping like some gigantic bird. "Who's the man?"

She laughed, a nervous bark. He looked ridiculous with his skinny limbs and caved-in chest but also, in a flickering, intermittent way, like his old self. Tall—she had forgotten that, how tall he was. Tall and almost stately, with his long, hooked nose and wide shoulders. The hospital light ringed his naked head like a crown.

"Tall king," she said in strange, dreamy voice. Immediately she saw that this was ridiculous, an absurd non sequitur.

He stopped and looked at her mockingly. "What did you say?"

119

It was him. It was her tall, funny husband. But it was him plundered, him eaten away. *Where has he gone?* she thought. *Where is my handsome young husband?* Grief burst open in her like a vein. For suddenly she saw: He was being taken, bit by bit; he was being taken and he would not come back.

"Did you say 'tall king'?" he said.

But she was already crying. He stepped over and pulled her up into him and she buried her face in his chest. She cried crazily, choking and spitting, not caring. When her sobs slowed, he took her face in his hands and kissed her forehead.

"Can we sit down?" he whispered.

He was shaking. Her tears stopped abruptly, as though a valve had been turned. "Sorry," she said.

She wrapped her arm under his shoulders and took his weight for the few steps to the bed. He let go of her and sat heavily; then he reached for her hand and pulled her down next to him. They leaned back against the raised mattress and turned their faces to the window. It was getting dark; the lights in the parking lot were coming on.

She watched the sharp line of his nose, the familiar bow of his lips. Her lungs were heavy and sodden but her mind was quiet, clear for the first time in a long while. She could feel the warm tangle of their life together, the days and weeks and years. He was alive in her the way her ribs were alive, and yet she would never know how it had been for him, all those weeks alone in bed—how he had thought about what lay ahead, while she was pretending.

A car started up in the parking lot, then another and another. *Shift change,* she thought. People going home or out to dinner or who knew where; going back to their lives. She listened to the cars accelerate one by one, thin lines of sound ascending into the darkness.

"Friday night," she said.

"Yep," he said. He squeezed her hand.

THE SOMEDAY CAT

Janie's brother Eddie said she was cross-eyed and that's why she wouldn't get adopted, but she wasn't; it was just the one eye that went off to the side sometimes. A lazy eye, her mother called it, and anyway it wasn't the reason. The reason was she was tough.

"You get any tougher your teeth are gonna come in pointy," her mother said.

Janie went to the bathroom mirror to see. There weren't any new teeth, just the bumpy red ridge where the two front ones hadn't grown in yet. She stared into her eyes and they stared back the same as always: brownish green with the black centers that opened into nothing, into the secret dark inside her head.

"Actually," she said to Jeremy on the picnic table later, "I don't *wanna* be adopted." Jeremy was only four and didn't matter, but she felt like telling someone.

"I could get 'dopted," Jeremy said.

"*A*-dopted," she said. "Go ahead, *I'm* not gonna. And anyway," she added, "adoption is for douche bags."

"I not a doose bag!" Jeremy cried.

"Are too."

Jeremy swung his feet in the gap between the tabletop and the seat. "Frank got 'dopted," he said slyly.

Janie shoved him.

"St-st-st-op!" he screamed. "Mommmmm!"

Their mother was inside, watching TV with the baby. They both sat still, listening, but the only sound was the wheezy chug-chug of the air conditioner in the living room window.

"Ha, ha," Janie hissed. She shoved him again just to get the itch out of her hands, then she jumped off the table and ran. She was planning to run around the house like an Olympic racer but it was too hot so she slowed to a walk and then to something that was maybe as fast as a bug would go—a slow bug or a bug with half its legs pulled off—but even this made her too hot, and at the kitchen steps she gave up and sat.

She didn't want to think about Frank.

—

She could still see him if she let herself, a tiny picture at the end of a tube, like when she looked the wrong way through the binoculars at school. Frank had been nice to her. He used to let her come and sit on his bed—not Melissa or Tommy or Eddie or Jeremy, just her. She would sit on the end of the bed and he would sit by the pillow and play his air guitar or tell her about the bands he liked or what he would do when he got famous from all his guitar playing, and sitting there, watching the tiny stars of dust float up and down and sideways in the light, Janie would feel everything inside her lie down and go quiet.

But one day that spring Frank had gotten into a fight with their mother's boyfriend. "Duane Lame-ass," Frank had called him, and everyone had laughed because it sounded so much like Duane Larasse, his real name. Then Duane had gotten mad and tried to hit Frank, but Frank had gotten tall, and when Duane tried to push him up against the wall, Frank put his hands around Duane's neck and shoved him into the fridge until Duane's face turned a fat-looking purple.

A few days later Janie came into the kitchen to find her mother reading something off a piece of paper. "'I am a single, white male with a steady job and a farm in the beautiful state of New Hampshire.'" She looked up at Frank. "A farm! Don't that sound nice?"

"What's that?" Janie said, grabbing for the paper.

Her mother snatched it out of reach. "Something Duane got off the computer. Get off!" She slapped Janie's hand away and kept reading. "'And I have room in my heart and my home for a young boy who needs a father. I lost my son to cancer two years ago and want to raise another boy to be a Godly and a Responsible young man.'"

"What boy?" Janie said. "Who got lost?"

No one answered. Her mother was looking at Frank; Frank was looking at the floor.

"I bet he's loaded," her mother said. "I bet he could buy you anything you want."

"I bet he could kiss my Godly and Responsible ass," Frank said, and Janie, relieved to see it was a joke, barked out a high, hooting laugh.

But when the farmer came a few days later, Frank didn't say anything at all; he just went upstairs and put his things in the plastic grocery bags Janie's mother gave him. In the back of the farmer's truck there was a new washing machine and a dryer in big cardboard boxes. Duane and the farmer dragged them off and pushed them down some boards into the basement; then Frank came out with his bags. Janie stood by the stairs to say goodbye, but Frank never looked back— he went to the truck and put in the plastic bags of his stuff and then he got in and shut the door without looking. Later he sent a picture of himself on his new bed. The farmer had bought him a guitar; you could see it in the picture.

Sometimes Janie would think she saw him and her heart would jump, but it was always just Eddie or a shadow or a lump of dirty clothes on the bed that was Jeremy's now, and for a second, standing there, she would feel all the color bleach out of the world.

Janie's mother told her to forget about him. "He ain't your brother anymore," she said. "He's got a new family now." She was feeding the baby in the kitchen.

Janie watched her stir the stinky baby cereal. A question was pressing inside her, heavy as a stone. "Let's get Jeremy adopted," she said.

"Nah, Jeremy's too little." Her mother put another spoonful in the baby's mouth. "Yum!" she said in a baby voice.

"Then who?"

"I dunno," her mother shrugged. "I guess it'd be Eddie, if it was anyone. Eddie or Melissa. They're oldest, anyhow."

"Not Tommy?"

"Did I say Tommy?"

The stone pressed in Janie's throat. "Not me?" she croaked.

"Did I say you?"

"Why not me?"

Duane put down his beer can. "Because you're such a little shit, that's why," he said.

"So?" Janie said, a bubble of relief blowing out, out in her chest. "So, you big fatso?"

Duane reached his arm out to smack her but Janie ducked out of the way and ran for the kitchen door yelling, "Fatso! Fatso!" and from the corner of her eye, she saw her mother's mouth curl up into a smile.

"You can't scare Janie," her mother said. "She's a tough ass like me."

—

That was back in the spring, when the air smelled sweet and the yard was covered in bright, soft grass. Now it was all just dirt and the only smell was the sour diaper stink of the garbage cans.

Janie stood up. The picnic table was deserted; Jeremy had gone inside. To tell on her probably, the big crybaby. She walked over and climbed onto the table's splintery top. Once she'd played pirates with Tommy on that table, and Marines down in the woods, where they could sneak up behind the mall and throw stones at the loading dock. But Tommy was twelve now and didn't play anymore. He was always with his girlfriend, Ashley, or down at the school yard playing basketball with his friends. He never even talked to Janie now unless she bugged him, and mostly what he said then was "Shut your face," like Eddie.

"Copycat," Janie muttered. She lay back and looked into the blazing, upside-down bowl of the sky. She was bored, bored, bored. Even her arms were bored, even her legs. She thought they might fall off from boredom. They might just unstring themselves and fall in the dirt. She tried to picture how it would be with no arms and legs. Would she have to roll down the stairs?

The screen door slapped shut. It was her mother. She had a dress on and she was holding the baby.

"I'm going out," she said. "You keep an eye on Jeremy."

Janie sat up. "Can I come?"

"No." She turned back toward the house. "Tommy! Get a move on!"

Tommy came out with a black trash bag. He had his head down and he was walking slow; his sneakers went scuff, scuff, scuff in the dirt.

"Jesus, would you move it?" her mother said. "I ain't got all day."

"How come Tommy gets to go?" Janie said.

"Mind your own beeswax." Her mother turned to open the car door and the baby's dumb baby face stared back at Janie over her shoulder. Janie stuck her tongue out but the baby just stared—she didn't know anything; she was just a dumb baby. Janie lay back down and listened to the car doors shut: slam, slam. Then the squealing of the engine and the sound of the car backing up and roaring forward down the street. Then nothing, the lazy drone of summer.

—

It never occurred to Janie that Tommy was gone, that her mother had come back with only the baby and a trunk full of groceries. In fact, when she ran inside and saw the plastic grocery bags slumped on the kitchen floor, her brain was too lit up with happiness to think of Tommy at all. There were

Pop-Tarts and Popsicles and Cocoa Krispies and pieces of corn wrapped up in plastic—there were so many things Janie couldn't even see them all.

Her older sister, Melissa, was taking everything out and putting it away. She gave Janie a look. "Don't even *think* about it," she said.

"And there's hot dogs," her mother was saying, "and hamburgs." She was sitting at the table with her legs up on a chair and she had a golden drink in a glass; the black-labeled bottle it came from was standing next to it. "And Doritos . . . I bought out the whole goddamn store."

Her words were slow and blurry at the edges; in fact, everything about her seemed to have softened. She was like Janie's Barbie when she put her in the bath and her hair floated and her clothes floated and she changed from a hard, pointy thing into something rippling and soft. This was the kind of mood in which her mother might do the unexpected—say yes or hug her or maybe even cry if they showed one of those animal stories on the news.

"Can I have a Popsicle?" Janie asked.

Her mother's eyes wandered over to her. "Go ahead, knock yourself out," she said, waving her hand sloppily in the air. "I got tons of everything."

"I have one, too!" Jeremy cried.

They waited while Melissa opened the box and grudgingly handed each of them a Popsicle. Janie stripped off the wrapper: grape. She put it in her mouth and went back to stand near her mother.

"And I got Honey Smacks," her mother was saying, "and that marshmallow cereal."

Janie walked in close; then, very slowly, she leaned against her mother's lap.

Her mother didn't push her off; she kept talking. "And deli chicken. D'you see that? We could have that tonight."

Janie breathed in the medicine smell of the drink and the sweat-and–baby powder smell that was her mother's. She was happy, leaning there—happy and jumpy in that ready-to-run way she always felt when her mother was nice. Slowly, the room began to fade. The words Melissa and her mother were saying became just sounds, like the wind or airplanes overhead. As the last sweet-cold lump of Popsicle slipped down her throat, she felt her lazy eye drift to the side like an empty boat. It was okay, she could rest; she could lean there in the comfortable, sleep-smelling scent that was her mother.

The door smacked open. Duane came in wearing his security guard uniform.

"Did you get it?" he said, throwing his keys on the counter.

Janie's mother reached over to fish an envelope out of her bag. "Oh, and I got those Ranch Doritos," she said. "Melissa? You hear me?"

Duane opened the envelope, pulled out a thick stack of

money and began to thumb through it. "This ain't all of it," he said. "Shannon! This ain't all of it."

"I know it ain't," she said. "What do you think I bought them groceries with, my looks?" She looked at Melissa and laughed, like it was a joke only Melissa would get.

Duane crossed his arms. Then, in his bad, quiet voice he said, "That ain't what we agreed on."

Suddenly Janie's mother slammed her drink on the table and jerked to her feet. "Was that *your* son, mister?" she yelled. She pointed her finger at Duane's face. "Was that your son just drove off with two strangers? Huh?" She started to tip and caught herself against the table. "You don't *know* what it's like watching one of your babies go. You don't have a fuckin' clue. So don't even *try* to talk to me."

"Who?" Melissa said, halfway to the cupboard with the bag of Doritos. "Who drove off?"

Her mother sat down and took another sip from her drink. "Tommy, honey," she said in a regular voice. "Tommy got adopted by a nice man from Boston and his wife."

There was a rushing in Janie's ears.

"Tommy got adopted?" Melissa said.

"That's what I said, ain't it?"

"But you said Eddie!" Janie cried. "You said it'd be Eddie or Melissa."

Melissa turned on her. "Oh, right! You wish!"

"But you *said*. You said because they were oldest—"

Janie's mother grabbed her arm and spun her around and Janie looked up into the cold of her eyes.

"I never said that," her mother said. All the softness had gone out of her. She was looking down at Janie and her eyes were mean. "Did I."

Janie's arm was thin as a stick inside the hard press of her mother's fingers. "No," she whispered.

"Anybody asks, you say Tommy's with his uncle. 'Cause that's where he is, he's with his nice aunt and uncle in Boston. Got it?"

Janie nodded.

Her mother let go of her with a little shove and sat down heavily in the chair. "They didn't want a teenager, anyhow," she said to Duane. "They would've took the baby if I'd've let 'em."

"Better the hell not," Duane said.

Janie stood very still, holding her arm. She could feel its flat thinness, and the hurt place where her mother's fingers had squeezed, and something else she had no words for: a crack or hole; a fast, cold drop into darkness.

———

The next morning, Janie's mother brought home the cat. A present, she said it was, a surprise present just for them. She'd bought it from some boys in the parking lot when she and Duane went to get the new TV. Everyone was standing in a knot by the front door looking at it when Janie came downstairs the next morning.

"So I said, 'Let's get something for the kids,' you know?" Janie's mother was saying. "Get you guys a treat." She broke off. "Aww, look at it!" she cooed.

"Awww!" Melissa said. "It's so cute!"

"I know, right?" Janie's mother said. She was leaning over the cat, smiling.

Not mad anymore, Janie saw; friendly. Suddenly she was excited, too. "Let me see!" she cried. But when she pushed past Jeremy to look, a tiny bolt of electricity struck her heart. The cat wasn't cute, it was ugly—ugly and small, with weak, spindly legs and patchy fur. And something else, which she seemed to see with the center of her chest: crooked eyes.

"But it's ugly!" she burst out. "It's a ugly cat!"

Her mother turned on her. "What?" she said. Her face had gone hard. "What'd you say?"

"Shut up, Janie!" Melissa said. "It's cuter than you anyway."

"Hey, it kinda looks like her," Eddie said. "See? It's got those messed-up eyes." He crossed his eyes and made zombie noises.

Janie's mother laughed; then Melissa laughed, too. Even Duane looked up from where he was unpacking the new TV to laugh at her.

A sound like the wind started up in Janie's head. "Shut up!" she cried.

"Shut up!" Eddie copied in a fake girl voice.

She was going to show him—kick him or hit him or yell in his face—but before she could move, something worse happened: The cat stood up on its rickety legs and began to stumble across the rug right toward her, just like she'd called it. "You shit!" she cried. "Get away from me!"

Eddie laughed. "Janie's scared of the cat."

"No I ain't!"

"Then why're you yellin' like that?" Melissa snorted. She bent down and scooped the cat up in her arms.

"Janie's a scaredy-cat," Eddie said. "Get it? Scaredy-cat?"

"I ain't scared!" Janie cried. But she didn't feel not scared; she felt trembly and weak, like anyone could push her over, even Jeremy.

—

The cat was called Someday. It was supposed to be Sundae, but Jeremy had come up with the name and "Someday" was the best he could say it. Janie's mother gave it a plate of pebble-shaped cat food and a bowl of water and Melissa made it a toy out of tinfoil and string.

Janie watched the cat flap its paws at the ball of tinfoil from her perch, high inside the kitchen doorframe. She'd climbed it by jamming her feet and hands flat against the wood—her "monkey trick," her mother called it—but today her mother hadn't even looked. She hadn't looked at or talked to Janie since the morning.

The cat stood up on its hind legs and whacked at the foil with both paws.

"Oh my God!" Melissa laughed.

"I know, right?" Janie's mother said. "It looks like a little bear or something."

Jealousy stung Janie. She would have liked to laugh at the cat, too, or wave the string around for it to bat at. But it was too late; she couldn't go back now. She pulled in her hands and feet and dropped to the floor. "Actually, I hate cats," she said.

"So?" Melissa said. "Stay away from her then."

Her mother blew out the smoke from her cigarette. "Damn well better," she said. Not to Janie, to the ceiling.

"I don't got to," Janie said. "You can't make me."

But her mother just turned her hand over and picked something off one of her fingernails.

"You can't make me," Janie said again.

Nothing, not even a look. It was like she wasn't even there.

Fear swept up in her, a crazy, panicked whirl. Her eyes landed on the cat, sitting all alone in the middle of the floor, and suddenly she saw what she could do. She rushed at it. For a split second, the cat's crooked eyes snagged on hers. She felt her foot hit the little body, saw it fly through the air. Then she heard her mother's chair scrape fast against the floor and she ran.

"Who cares," Janie muttered under the picnic table. She hated them, anyway: her mother and Melissa. The cat, too—she'd kick it again if she got a chance. But the idea of kicking the cat, which had felt so right, was mixed up now with the sound it had made, that little *meep* of hurt and surprise, and she didn't want to think about it.

"Who cares," she said again. She could live out there if she had to. She could make a bed under the picnic table and sneak in to steal food, and if her mother came after her, she could run out to the woods, climb a tree. She glanced over at the screen door—still shut.

Maybe her mother had forgotten; maybe she wasn't going to come after her at all.

Suddenly, Janie couldn't sit there anymore. She crawled out from under the table and sprinted across the yard, quiet as a spy. Find her mother, she was thinking; make her look. She tiptoed up the stairs to the back porch and pressed her face against the dust-smelling screen.

Her mother was in there, talking on the phone. "No, you can't," she was saying. "A deal's a deal."

Janie heard the faint voice on the other end of the line rise into a wail.

"Stop being such a crybaby," her mother said. "Did you see Frank crying? Huh? Did you?"

Tommy.

Her mother was tucking the phone under her chin, shaking a cigarette out of her pack. She put it between her fingers to light; then suddenly she seemed to forget about the cigarette, she let her hand drop and started shouting. "I ain't your mother anymore! Get it through your head!" Then: "I'm hanging up now. Tommy, I'm hanging up!" She took the phone away from her ear, pushed the button, and threw it down on the table.

Janie watched her fumble with the lighter: rasp click, rasp click. After a few tries, she threw that down, too, and lit the cigarette from the stove. Then she just stood there with her shoulders bent, smoking and staring at the floor.

Something tugged in Janie; she put her hand on the door to yank it open.

Her mother's eyes jerked up and saw her. "What're *you* looking at, you little shit?"

Janie felt the fear whirl up. "I can look," she squeaked.

"*'I can look,'*" her mother imitated. "You better not be coming in here, you hear me? And don't even *think* about bugging that cat."

The cat. Janie spun around: It was there, right behind her, sitting on the top step. She hadn't even seen it. "I could bug it!" she cried, turning back to her mother. "I could bug it if I want!"

Her mother's narrowed eyes glinted at her through the smoke of her cigarette.

"I could bug it!" Janie said again. "See?" She ran at the cat and it shot into the yard. "See?" she yelled over her shoulder as she chased after it, but there was no answer, and when she looked back, she saw that the screen door was dark—her mother had gone.

Her legs dragged to a stop. Around her, the yard stretched out like a desert, flat and empty under the hot glare of the sun. And in the middle, like a terrible message just for her, the cat.

It was hunched over itself in a patch of dead grass, sucking its sides in and out, and a horrible sound was coming out of it, a gross, scraping hack. "You gross!" Janie cried. "Shut up!" But the cat didn't shut up; it kept lurching and gagging, lurching and gagging, until Janie couldn't stand it, she had to make it stop.

She ran over and hit it across the thin grille of its ribs. The cat skidded across the dirt; then it scrambled up, pitched forward, and vomited a string of bubbly spit.

Sick.

Janie's breath caught. Her mother would think she'd done it, she'd made it sick. She looked around to check if anyone had seen and then she stood up and scurried away, her heart crouched down like when she ran across the top of the monkey bars at school, a dizzy drop of air on either side.

—

"I dunno," she'd say if anyone asked her, "I ain't seen it." She stared up at the thin slashes of light in the top of the picnic table. Maybe a shrug? She splayed her hands, help-less. Inside the house, the phone started ringing again. Janie abandoned the shrug and put her fingers in her ears. *Two,* she counted, *three.*

The phone had been ringing all afternoon. At first her mom had answered it so she could yell at Tommy to stop calling, but now she wouldn't even pick it up and if you so much as walked near it, she'd scream at you. *Twenty-one, twenty-two.* Janie's arms were getting tired. *Twenty-three.* She gave up and let her hands fall back down. The phone gave one last, choked-off ring and stopped.

Quiet now; she could play if she wanted. But she couldn't, she was thinking about the cat again.

She crawled out from under the table and began to walk slowly along the edge of the house, her legs dragging through the heavy air. Not under the bushes, not behind the garbage cans, not in the suffocating gloom under the back stairs. She didn't want to find the cat. She didn't want to see its little body freeze or raise her hand and hit it or sneak away afterward with that bad, wobbly feeling inside. But she had to. Even if she was playing something, even if she was too hot to move, the idea of it would come to her and she'd have to go find it.

Not by the driveway, not under the front porch. She was just about to turn away and quit when she spotted it: a flash of gray under the evergreen bush by the front door. The jolt went through her chest. "You shit!" she gasped.

She lay down on her belly and began to pull herself over

the powdery, needle-flecked dirt. The cat was in the back, a raggedy ball of fluff by the stone foundation of the house. Bent around itself. Licking. Janie blinked and looked again. No, not licking—biting—biting its own stomach.

Fear surged up in her and she shoved her arm across the dirt and poked it hard in the side.

—

That night, when Melissa was handing out the hot dogs, the phone started ringing again and Janie's mother blew up.

"That's it!" she yelled. "That is fuckin' *it!*" She stomped over and pulled the plug out of the wall. "Any of you so much as *touches* that plug, you're outta here." She glared around at them. "Out! You hear me?"

Melissa said it wasn't fair; what if her friends were trying to call her?

"Ask me if I care," Janie's mother said, sitting back down. "Go ahead. Ask me."

Melissa didn't ask her. She just stood there with her arms folded and her chin jutted out like she was going to fight someone.

Jeremy was tipped sideways on his seat, looking under the table. "Where Someday?" he asked.

Melissa looked at Janie. "Where's the cat at?"

"I dunno," Janie said, but her voice came out wrong, shaky-sounding.

"Did you do something to it?" Melissa demanded. Her eyes were skinny and hard. "*Did* you, you little shit?"

"No!" Janie said.

"Better get off your ass and find it," her mother said.

Janie tried to concentrate on her hot dog—the juicy pop of its skin, the red, meaty flavor—but she couldn't taste a thing.

—

When Janie woke up the next morning, she couldn't remember at first why she had the sick, hollow feeling in her stomach. Then it came to her: the cat. She lay there, staring at the ceiling with the bad feeling spreading out inside her until she had another thought, a better one: Cocoa Krispies. If she didn't get down there, Jeremy might eat them all.

She jumped up and pulled on her shorts from the day before. Maybe the cat had come back on its own, she thought. It might have gotten better in the night; it might be in the kitchen right now, eating its gross pebble food. She gave the cat's bowl a sideways glance as she skipped through the kitchen: still full. Flies were sitting on it. She looked away.

Melissa was at the table; the box of Cocoa Krispies was right next to her. Janie ran over and dug her hand in—lots left, enough for two bowls at least. But just as her fingers were closing around a fat handful, Melissa snatched it away. Cocoa Krispies scattered across the floor.

"You wanna eat," Melissa said, "you better find that cat."

"Give it to me!" Janie cried, jumping for the box.

"Find that cat, you little shit," Melissa said.

"I'm hungry!" Janie wailed.

Melissa gazed at her, hesitating.

"Please!" Janie said.

"Okay, put your hands out," she said grudgingly. She scooped out some cereal and dropped it in Janie's palms. Then she held the box up out of the way again. "Now go get that cat."

The air was hot and hard to push through. Janie shuffled around the perimeter of the house, crunching the chocolaty taste in her teeth. Past the trash cans and the pricker bush, past the place where the hose hooked up. With a little thrum of dread, she stopped at the evergreen bush. She didn't want to look. She stood there for a minute, trying to think of a way out. Then her stomach growled and she gave up and dropped to her knees to peer under.

It was still there, lying flat by the wall of the house, its tail resting in a yellowish pool of yuck. Janie lowered herself onto her belly and scooched toward it. The cat didn't even look at her; it just lay there with its ribs jerking up and down. *Sleeping*, she thought. But when she crawled in a little farther, she saw that there were raw, red bulges in the corners of its eyes, like something that belonged inside was squeezing out.

Something terrible was going to happen.

She scrambled out from under the bush. *Find someone, play something*, she thought. She ran around the house, into the backyard. Jeremy was there, digging in the ground with a plastic shovel. He had a square pile of dirt, all patted together, and a hole he was digging to get more.

Janie stopped next to him. "Whatcha making?" she gasped.

"House," he mumbled.

"Can I play?"

He didn't answer.

Fear moved like a fish in her belly. "Come on, move over. Let me play."

Jeremy dropped the shovel and let his arms fall down.

She snatched for breath. "What're you stopping for?"

He shrugged.

"You think I'm gonna wreck it? I ain't gonna wreck it."

He had his head bent forward like someone was going to hit him.

"Say something!" Janie yelled. Everything was broken up and ragged and she couldn't breathe. "*Say* something, you stupid!"

But Jeremy didn't say anything, he just ducked his head under his arm, and she jumped up and smashed her feet down on his house.

—

Janie zigzagged across the yard like a pinball in slow motion—bush to picnic table to kitchen to bush. Every time she checked, the cat was still lying there, jerking its ribs up and down. When the kitchen was empty, Janie snuck in and got some food and a cup of water. But the cat wouldn't eat or even move and when she picked its head up and held it over the water, its head just flopped down and splashed the water into the dust.

Bush to table to kitchen to bush. After a while, the cat's ribs stopped jerking. It looked flat, in the shadow of the bush; Janie could hardly make it out. She straightened up and walked back to the kitchen. Melissa was in there; she couldn't go in. She turned away and walked back to the picnic table, then over to the bush. Something invisible was winding, tighter and tighter.

Later, when Janie finally crawled back under the bush to check, the cat's eyes were dull as old marbles. She reached her hand out and touched its leg: it was hard, like wood—wood with fur pasted on. As she watched, a couple of flies came and landed on its eyes. They poked with their poker things: eating them.

Terror gripped her. She forgot about not telling. She backed out of the bush and ran up the steps and into the kitchen. Melissa was in there, smoking one of their mother's cigarettes and talking on the phone.

"It's sick!" Janie cried. "The cat! It's sick, you gotta help!"

For a second, Melissa just stared at her. Then she jumped like she'd been slapped and let the phone clatter to the floor.

"It's sick!" Janie wailed, but Melissa had already run outside, the screen door smacked shut behind her.

A voice drifted up from the phone, thin as a thread. "Hello? Melissa?"

Janie bent down and picked up the phone and then suddenly her mother was coming, fast and angry, like something out of a bad dream.

She snatched the phone out of Janie's hand. "Who is this?" she said into it. "Department of *what*? Tommy who? No. *No*, okay? You got the wrong number. No!" She pressed the hang-up button and turned around.

Run, Janie thought, but she couldn't move.

Her mother grabbed her by the shoulders. "What'd you tell her?" she hissed. "Huh? What'd you say to that woman?" Her fingernails were digging into Janie's skin. "Tell me, you little shit!"

But Janie's body had gone stiff; she couldn't speak.

Her mother pushed her away and straightened up. "Shit!" she cried. She put her hand to her forehead. "Shit! What am I gonna tell Duane?"

She dropped her hand and looked back at Janie with hard eyes. "You're next. You hear me? I'm telling Duane you're next."

—

The cop car came down the road slowly, like it didn't really care. Cops, not a nice man and woman like Tommy had or a farmer like Frank. Because of the crimes she'd done to the cat, Janie knew, but she was too tired to care. She stood by the window and watched as the car ambled into the cul-de-sac and made the lazy turn around. Melissa had already washed Janie's hair with the lice soap and put her clothes in the grocery bags and now she was to stay in her room or else. Once she wouldn't have listened, she would have taken off into the woods, but her legs had gone dead on her—her legs and her arms and the middle of her, too—they were stiff and dumb as wood. And anyway, it was too late; her mom had said so.

The cop car stopped in front of the house and the engine cut off. For a long moment, nothing else happened. Then the doors opened and two cops got out, a fat one and a thin. Now another car was coming, a regular one. It pulled up behind the cop car and tried to park, jerking forward, going back. Then it stopped, too, and a Black man got out, then a Black lady. Now all four of them were turning, walking up the path.

Janie's pulse started to race inside the dead of her body. Downstairs, there was a flimsy knock on the screen door, a woman's voice calling, "Hellooo!"

Maybe no one would hear them, Janie thought; maybe her mother had changed her mind. But no, she could hear someone talking to them now—Melissa, it sounded like. Janie heard the squeal of the screen door being pulled back.

Coming for her.

She cracked open the door and stood behind it, listening.

"Let's pack up a few of your favorite outfits, okay?" someone was saying. "You got a favorite T-shirt?"

"Yeah."

That was Jeremy, Janie could tell; only why was *he* packing? She slipped out the door and crept to the top of the stairs. It was the Black lady talking to Jeremy; she was leaning over so her face was down by his.

"Or a favorite toy?" she said.

The woman's voice was as smooth and dark as her skin. *Like chocolate*, Janie thought. She let her feet slide down over the edge of the top step and land with a bump on the next one.

The woman looked up. "Oh, is this your other sister? Hi! I'm Deanna. What's your name?"

Melissa took the cigarette out of her mouth. "That's Janie," she muttered.

Janie let her feet slide down a few more stairs.

"Janie? Short for Jane?" the woman was saying. "Now that's pretty, you know? That's a *classic*. Well, Janie, you're gonna come away with me for a few days, okay? So I need you to pack up a few things—a couple a shirts and shorts, some PJs, a special toy if you want. But don't worry too much about toys and things 'cause we got plenty, okay?"

From the second-to-last stair, Janie watched the woman's lips stretch open in a smile. She seemed like a nice lady, the kind who might give her things, but the words she was saying didn't make sense. "You got toys at jail?" she asked softly.

"What's that, honey?" the woman said. "Oh, excuse me a sec."

Janie watched her as she walked over to the living room and leaned in the doorway. There was a pause, like the air was holding its breath. Then suddenly the baby started screaming.

Janie ran to the doorway. Her mother was in there, holding the wailing baby, and the Black man was right in front of her.

"You ain't takin' my baby," her mother said.

Everyone started talking at once—the woman, the cops—but Janie's mother wasn't listening, she was staring at the man, her eyes narrowed. "Whatcha gonna do, big man?" she was saying. "Huh? You gonna take my baby?"

The fat cop stepped forward. "I'm gonna get her arm," he said. "Then you get the baby, okay?" He walked up behind Janie's mother and grabbed one of her arms. Then, very slowly, he began to bend it up behind her back.

A shock went through Janie. That was her mother with her arm bent up; that was her mother they were hurting.

She felt her mind, her limbs unstiff themselves. Now the Black man was stepping toward her mother; he was towering right over her. Janie's body drew together, like an arrow in its bow.

The man reached his arms out, his fingers open to grab, and Janie threw herself into the air, claws outstretched, a crazy cat scream ripping through her mouth.

YOU THE ANIMAL

Jared didn't say he hated his job at the Department of Children and Families. He said it was time for a change, which sounded professional and mature and brought to mind his recent engagement and the financial responsibilities that would entail. As his future in-laws had taken to saying, he and Eliana would never be able to pay their bills if they were both saving the world, and she wasn't about to give up teaching art in the New Haven public schools. Besides, Jared had just been accepted to law school. He'd be crazy to pass up that kind of an opportunity, he thought, looking around at the shabby office he shared with his supervisor, Deanna.

"You sure the brother didn't just go to a relative's for the summer?" Deanna was saying into the phone. "You're *not* sure. Uh-huh." She swiveled her chair around to roll her eyes at him, the receiver still pressed to her ear.

One of *those* calls. Jared shook his head at her in a show of commiseration. He didn't really feel it, though. He didn't feel much of anything about DCF now, aside from an overpowering desire to leave it behind. But Deanna would have been hurt if she knew that, and he wouldn't have hurt her for the world. She was the reason he'd given two months' notice when he could have gotten away with two weeks—two days, even. Hell, he could have walked out at lunch and never come back. People at the DCF had been known to do that. Leave a Post-it on the computer screen, grab your personal items, and—poof—outta there. But that wasn't him; he wasn't a shirker. He lived up to his responsibilities, whether he liked them or not.

He looked again at the case files lying on his desk: nineteen neat bundles of chaos and despair. The sight of them gave him a compulsive urge to do something else—check email, text Eliana, put his head on the desk and sleep.

—

In the beginning, Jared had assumed that he would care deeply about his "families," as they were called. He had pictured himself bringing the kids to the movies, having heart-to-hearts with the parents, guiding them all back to safety and sense. Deanna did that, was that. She called the moms on their birthdays and took the kids out for meals; found out who needed money for a prom dress or a basketball uniform and made sure they got it. She never seemed to feel disgusted or discouraged; she just went in and sorted it out—who needed rehab, who needed counseling, who could take the children. If there was no rehab spot, there was no rehab spot, what could she do? Maybe one would open up later. She found whatever sliver of hope there was and held on to it: a clean drug test, a good report card, a little plastic Happy Meal toy one of the kids had given her. "Now, how about that?" she would say, the shine in her eyes untainted by doubt.

What Jared felt was more like horror and then, over time, a growing impatience. Because who could help these people? Deanna had just filed a ninety-six-hour hold on a baby who had been scalded by her teenage mother—a girl who turned out to be one of four children Deanna had removed from a home ten years earlier, when she was a skinny eight-year-old dotted from the neck down with the burn marks of cigarettes.

"Mmm mmm mmm," Deanna had said when she recognized the girl's name, the soft brown skin at the corners of her mouth puckering. But ten minutes later she was putting on her lipstick, asking if Jared wanted to go to KFC. He went, of course—he always went, even when he wasn't hungry—and he ate, too. There was something about being with Deanna that calmed him. He loved to sit across the table from her and watch her arrange her food in her deliberate, dainty way. She was a big woman, not so much fat as soft, with a heavy chest and a comfortable roll of flesh above her belt. Had he thought about it, he would have realized she'd been beautiful once; the evidence was still there in her high cheekbones, her rich, red-brown skin. But it wasn't beauty that held him, it was the signs of her aging: the little sags of flesh under her jaw, a huskiness in her voice that spoke of a wisdom accrued, one hard year after another, like layers of opalescent shell. She seemed to him to have a kind of earned and unimpeachable rightness that only women like her could claim, and he had a childish wish to save her from some sort of threat or trouble. He imagined her walking home in Newhallville, the black section of New Haven where she lived, walking home tired and alone, and some scumbag coming out of the darkness to mug her—a young black man was what he pictured, with a rush of outrage.

Of course, he himself had been a young black man in that neighborhood once. Or at least that was how any stranger would have seen him. The fact that his mother was white was something people didn't usually guess, dark as he was.

"Your daughter said— Uh-huh," Deanna was saying. "Well, you know, that's kids. Let me explain what we do. Our job is to investigate suspected abuse or neglect, okay? Now, the first step is to report your concerns, as you are doing now. Then, my colleagues and I will conduct what we call a preliminary investigation to determine whether abuse or neglect is in fact— What? No? So it's just that she thinks he's been sent . . . and the brother. Maybe the brother. Okay. Well, tell you what, why don't I give the school a call, see what they know. And you get back to me if you hear anything more, okay? Sure. All right. You take care now."

Jared heard her place the phone back in its cradle. "C and I?" he asked. "Conjecture and Innuendo" was their name for calls that gave them nothing to go on—no facts, no witnessed events, sometimes not even a name or address.

"Mmm-hmm."

He turned his head to look at her. "What's the allegation?"

"Well—that's a good question." She scanned the pad she'd been writing on. "Okay, so this mother, the one who called, she says her daughter's twelve-year-old boyfriend told her—told the daughter, I mean—that he's been sent away to live with someone he doesn't know."

He waited but she was silent, reading her notes. "That's it?"

"Uh-huh. And I guess that another brother was sent away last spring, also to live with someone he didn't know."

"Someone like a relative?"

She looked at him over the top of her leopard-print drugstore reading glasses. "See?"

"You mean C and I," Jared said, and they both laughed. She had a great laugh, Deanna.

"Mmm mmm mmm," she said, drumming her long nails on the desk. They were still painted like the American flag, the design she'd chosen for the Fourth a couple of weeks back. "Well," she sighed, "maybe I'll give the school a call, see if they know anything. Better safe than sorry, you know?"

"I hear you," Jared said. The previous winter, after months of anxious deliberation, the department had returned a seven-year-old girl to her parents only to have her body turn up in a Dumpster a few weeks later. No one was taking any chances after that.

He pulled out the notes from his interview with Porsche Rivera and laid them on the desk. Will, their department head, had called that morning to ask for his report. Now that Porsche was pregnant again, they were going to conduct a comprehensive review of her case. All Jared had to do was type up Porsche's answers and write a few paragraphs describing her "demeanor," "appearance," and "apparent emotional state." Easy enough. He had been putting it off, though, for nearly two weeks.

He filled his cheeks with air as he read over his notes. They were in a sorry state—sloppy, almost disturbed-looking. He'd have to throw them out after he finished the report.

Cover his tracks.

No, that wasn't right—he hadn't done anything wrong. Why should he be defensive? Porsche was the one who'd screwed up. *Just get it done,* he thought. He let the trapped breath shoot through his lips and opened a new document on his computer.

—

When Jared first started at the DCF, Deanna had tried to talk to him about growing up in Newhallville, but the conversations never went anywhere. It wasn't so much that Deanna was twenty years older as that they didn't know anyone in common. Or, more accurately, that Jared didn't know anyone. He hadn't been allowed to play outside as a child, and his parents had pretty much kept to themselves—or maybe people had shunned them, he wasn't sure which. In any case, it wasn't something Deanna would have understood. She was a real Newhallville resident, the kind of person he and his mother had seen sitting on the porches as they walked silently home. How comfortable and happy they'd looked, leaning loose-limbed against the railings, talking and laughing and teasing. He could have reached out and touched them, he passed so close, and yet he could no more have joined them than flown to the moon.

The reasons for this were too shameful to tell anyone, let alone Deanna. But one day, shortly after the engagement party at Eliana's parents' place in Philadelphia, Jared had found himself telling her anyway. Not just about his mother and her crazy ways but also things he had never told anyone, even Eliana: his father's rages and his mother's taunting and the last, surreal fight that had sent his mother to the hospital and his father to jail and Jared to three muffled, friendless years at his maternal grandparents' house in suburban Massachusetts. It all came spewing out; he couldn't stop himself. He didn't even *want* to stop, once he got started; it was such a relief to finally tell someone.

A peculiar stillness had come over Deanna's face as he talked, as though she were receding behind her features. It occurred to him as he babbled on, too deep in to change course, that this might be the end of their camaraderie, that the warm sense of belonging she had extended to him might be withdrawn. Later, driving home, he saw it more starkly: He had revealed himself as the outsider he really was. Now he would be exiled, shut out by the same invisible screen that came down behind Deanna's eyes with people she didn't trust. White people, mostly, like Will, their boss.

Jared had spent that night in a state of secret terror. Everything his mind touched on seemed to be ringed with fear, even Eliana. At any moment, it seemed to him, the life he had built would swing back like a stage set and leave him in darkness.

In fact, nothing changed. Deanna never mentioned what he'd told her; she didn't even indicate that she remembered it, although she did stop talking to him about growing up in Newhallville. She went on treating him the way she always had—like a brother or a nephew, one of her own.

At first, Jared had felt a shaken, almost tearful gratitude over this. Later, it began to seem like his right. He'd worked hard to make a life for himself. Why should his parents, his childhood, have any bearing on who he was now?

—

"That Porsche's?" Deanna asked.

"Yep," Jared said cheerfully, as he stuffed the single sheet into an interoffice envelope. Relief was already buoying him.

"She come a long way, you know? When you think how she came up, with her mother and all."

"Uh-huh," Jared said.

"She still with that boyfriend?"

"Uh-huh." Then, as though to shrug off an invisible constraint: "Some dogs can't learn, you know?" Too late, he heard how that sounded.

But the rueful half smile Deanna turned on him was free of judgment. "Well, you know me," she said, "always hoping."

Instantly, he felt the release, the sudden enlargement of space he so often experienced around her. "We wouldn't have it any different, D," he said, warmly.

"Oh, go on," she said, but he could tell she was tickled. "Anyway, she young. She got time to work it out," she added.

Jared was saved from responding by the sudden buzz of his phone—a text from Eliana. She was waiting out front.

"I gotta go," he said. "You have yourself a good night, okay?"

He took the stairs three at a time, shoved open the old school door with its chicken-wire glass. Eliana was parked in front of the fire hydrant. *Typical,* he thought. She had an instinctive disdain for rules. He gazed at her hungrily as he walked around to the passenger side. Even in a tank top, even sitting in that busted-up old car, she looked slender-necked and queenly, a Nefertiti with dreads. He threw his bag in the back and got in.

She looked up, leaned over to kiss him. "Hey," she said.

"Hey," he whispered, already lost in the smell of her.

—

The trouble with Porsche had come out of the blue. She wasn't even Jared's case; they had just needed someone who wasn't her regular caseworker to follow up on some new information they'd received, or so he'd been told. He'd scheduled the interview for a Monday, a beautiful day, as it turned out, warm but not humid, with a blue, boundless summer sky. Good weather for a dinner at the shore, was what he'd been thinking on the drive over—leave work a little early maybe, take Eliana to that outdoor seafood place in Guilford he'd heard so much about. Good thoughts, happy thoughts, which he was still turning over in his mind as he climbed the front stairs to Porsche's new apartment, a first floor across the street from New Hope Baptist.

The apartment looked nice enough, clean and organized, with her sons' pictures up on the fridge and a pair of twin beds on display in the only bedroom. The beds, Jared noticed, were neatly made and piled high with cheap stuffed animals, as though the boys might be coming home at any minute. He looked away, his good mood evaporating. What had Will said? "Get her side of the story." But also: "Confirm what's in the reports." And if he was able to do that . . . A shadow fell over his mind. He reached up to pull his collar away from his neck, as though it were choking him.

Porsche was standing in front of the stove, one tawny hand on her swollen belly. Her hair had been professionally braided and her large, amber eyes were carefully outlined in black. *Island eyes*, Jared thought as he took a seat at the kitchen table. Her mother was African American but her father, he knew, had been Puerto Rican. That was normal now, a mixed background; people hardly even commented on it. Not like when he was growing up. And he was only what—six years older than her? Seven?

"You want some coffee or somethin'?" Porsche asked softly.

He shook his head. For some reason, he found the offer irritating. But then everything was suddenly irritating him: the stuffed animals and the pictures on the fridge and the pungent smell of the cleaner on the still-damp kitchen floor— the whole, frantic effort. He opened his bag, removed the police report, and laid it in front of her.

Her young face sagged.

"So," Jared said, suppressing the weird smile that had sprung to his mouth, "as your caseworker—Peggy McClaren, right?—okay, as Peggy no doubt told you, there's going to be a comprehensive review of your case. But first, you and I need to get straight on a few things. A few facts, okay?" He sounded all right, he thought: professional, in control. Will would have approved. "First, this police report. Now, you told Peggy you were admitted to the hospital because you fell down the stairs. Is that what really happened?"

Porsche opened her mouth to speak and then closed it. Almost imperceptibly, she shook her head.

"So the real story—correct me if I'm wrong," he said, "the real story is that you and your boyfriend at the time, Dante Rodriguez, right? So you and Dante were walking down Bassett Street, when he was witnessed"—he turned the police report around and scanned it for the exact wording—"striking you and knocking you down, and then dragging you by your shirt and/or hair along the sidewalk as far as Newhall Street, where he was apprehended by Officer Reginald Bryant and placed under arrest." He looked up at her. "Is this what happened?"

"It's just—he just get a little rough sometime," she said.

"Is this or is this not what happened?" he asked, calmly.

"I guess. I mean, if that's what they saying." Her wide face was as passive and expressionless as a cow's.

She looked like the kind of girl a man would hit.

Jared averted his eyes. A pressure was building in his chest, an outward-pushing tension, like what he'd felt as a kid when he held his breath too long underwater. He pulled at his collar and plowed on. "So that sounds like 'yes, he did hit you,' causing you the injuries for which you were then treated at Yale New Haven." Without looking at her for confirmation, he began to write this answer down. The pen dragged against the paper—running out. He pressed down harder: y-e-s. "And are you still involved with Dante Rodriguez?"

"Dante the father of my baby," she said in a helpless voice. As if it weren't up to her.

"So you're still involved with him," he said.

"Yeah. I mean, mostly, I guess."

"So I'm going to put that down as a yes." In a kind of rage, he carved "YES" into his notepad with the nearly inkless pen. "Now, as you may recall, a drug test was performed while you were in the hospital. That test came out positive for cocaine. Here's the results right here." He took the second paper out of his bag and laid it on top of the police report. "Do you recall getting high on cocaine that day?"

Tears were welling up in her golden eyes.

"I'm going to need an answer," he said.

"Okay, yeah," she whispered.

"So that's 'yes,'" he said. "And are you currently taking drugs?"

"No!" she cried. "No, I'm clean, I swear."

"You're clean," he repeated, not bothering to hide his disbelief.

"Look, I messed up. I *know* I messed up but that was just one time! Outta all the days I done right, all the days I done exactly what I'm supposed to, that was my one and only mess-up and now I'm back on track with it, I really am. You got to believe me!"

Full-on crying now. Jesus.

"Just ask my counselor! *She* know. She see me comin' in for the meetings. Please, you got to ask her, you got to hear the good. All you got is the bad, the mess-up. You got to—"

"I don't 'got to' anything," Jared said. "All I 'got to' do

is report the facts, which is precisely what I'm doing right now." He etched "Claims to be drug-free" into his pad and stood up.

Porsche clasped her hands together. "Please, I can't give up my kids, I just can't," she cried. "No one else gonna be Momma to them, not in they minds. I'm the only one. And I'm tryin', I really am. You got to believe me!" Her face looked almost obscene, the pain in it was so vivid.

Jared shoved the papers back into his bag. Now would have been the time to wrap up the interview, say, "Your caseworker will follow up with you," or even "Good luck." But he said nothing; he slung his bag over his shoulder and made for the door.

Why he was shaking as he walked out into the brightness of the street, why his heart felt like an unpinned grenade, were questions he didn't ask himself.

—

What got to him, he told himself later, was how she hadn't really tried. You saw it all the time with these DCF families—that hopeless passivity, that utter failure to change. In idle moments, Jared sometimes thought about how he might put together a lecture or a workshop on this—tell it like it really was, light a fire under a few butts. Because the truth was you *could* determine the shape of your own life. He'd done it himself.

It was during the darkest period of his life, when he was fifteen and living with his maternal grandparents. He didn't mind telling people about it, if the subject came up: how all on his own he'd figured out what he wanted to be and set about achieving that—without parents or role models, without even a friend.

What he didn't want to tell anyone, couldn't even really let himself remember, was the fear.

During the day, he had been all right: sitting with his not-quite-friends at lunch, walking the lonely mile home to his grandparents', dropping his eyes when anyone looked his way so that no one would feel threatened. Even the house was okay in the daytime. There were no rages, no twisted, hopeless talks. His grandparents greeted him politely, cooked him three meals a day, spoke in measured tones about neutral topics, like sports or the weather. Everything was orderly and quiet, as muffled as Jared's own footsteps on the thickly carpeted floors.

He did his best to play along—do what they did, say only things they might say—and, in this way, he managed to skim through the days. But at night, as he lay awake in his grandparents' spare bed, this cardboard, daylight self would fall away, and a cold tide of fear would flood him. He did not belong; he was rattling, like a broken satellite, through the limitless dark.

As a child, when he was upset, Jared had made himself feel better by building things—planes, models of famous buildings, *Star Wars* ships. He would study the plan on its thin, cheaply printed paper, thinking through each step. This was pure pleasure, once he could calm down and focus—his mind was good at converting the flat diagrams into three-dimensions, seeing the reason and sense behind the tiny, cryptic words. At first, the construction would look pathetic, even shameful, one more thing his father could deride him for. But if he kept going, if he made his decisions with care, he could build something that withstood all that—a form, marvelously complete and sufficient unto itself.

One night, as he lay in bed, stiff with fear, it occurred to him that a life might be built, too. But what plan could he follow? He didn't know anyone like himself, with a black, failed writer father and a mentally ill mother. The next evening, watching football with his grandfather, he swallowed his pride and spoke into the hard-packed silence.

"How do you become a success?" he asked. The question sounded childish, laughable.

"A success, huh?" his grandfather said, and though his tone was gruff, perhaps even mocking, something in his expression told Jared he was pleased. The answer he gave was simple enough: get into a good college; join a fraternity; choose a respectable profession and stick to it.

His grandfather had gone to Amherst, so that was the name Jared dropped when he went to see the college counselor at school the next day. To his surprise, the counselor, a middle-aged white man, was encouraging, though when

Jared got out a pad and pen and asked what steps he should take, he saw the man suppress a smile. But Jared was too scared to be self-conscious. He asked his question again, and the plan, as written that morning in the counselor's office, went up on the wall above his desk. By his senior year, he had checked off everything on that list, from the 4.0 GPA through the three years of Latin and the not-too-popular sport (fencing). The acceptance letter from Amherst affected him like a revelation: He had decided what course his life should take, and lo and behold, it had taken that course.

In the first flush of his triumph, Jared requested a room in the African American "theme dorm." Why not? He certainly qualified. But on the first day of school, when he arrived at the base of the building's grand entryway, his heart sank. A small crowd of students was gathered on the porch, gesturing and talking over each other, some of them standing, some sitting, all of them a shade of brown.

A mistake, he saw, a foolish overreach. He'd never fit in.

One of the girls cried out, "Muh!" and the argument dissolved into laughter. Then she looked over and saw him, frozen on the bottom stair.

"Hi," she said, rising, "I'm Jacqui." She was freckled and latte-pale, but she belonged, Jared could see it in the comfortable way she turned and scolded the others: "Y'all got no manners, you know that? Get off your butts and say hello."

"Chill, girl. We're coming," a boy said, and then they

all stood up and wandered over to meet him, jostling and teasing and laughing.

Jared had never wanted anything the way he wanted to be part of that.

He had brought all the wrong clothes, knew all the wrong music, could not for the life of him think of anything to say. Over time, though, the house worked its magic on him. The conversations and laughter, the casual brilliance with which his dorm mates spun out jokes and coined new words ("Muh," was one of these), blew like a current of fresh air through all the shut places in him. He learned what to wear, relaxed enough to speak, began to see what might be of value in himself—his memory, a certain precision of thought, even, for the first time in his life, the way he looked.

He went back to his grandparents' house less and less—his mother was living there now, and seeing him seemed to set her off. And so the old, bitter trap of his childhood began to recede, and he found to his amazement that he was free to choose his own path.

That path was already clear to him: law school, marriage, a judgeship, if he played his cards right. So why did he put it off to work at DCF? If anyone asked him, he always said he'd wanted to "give back" and left it at that. The real reason was something he couldn't put into words—a nagging, embarrassed feeling, as though he'd screwed up all those years ago in New Haven, needed to go back, set the record straight. What record, and for whom, he never got around to figuring out. He rented an apartment, took the job at DCF, settled in.

—

Jared knew that the Porsche thing had to resurface. Still, he was taken by surprise when Will's email arrived. It was another hot day, one of a string of them, which the weather-people were now saying would continue at least through the end of the week. The kids in the neighborhood had begun busting open fire hydrants, and the sheets of water pulsing across the street looked nearly as tempting to Jared now as they had when he was a child, sweltering in their little living room while the other kids shrieked and splashed outside. He was doing all right, though. He'd gotten straight to work that morning, made a few phone calls, written up a case summary. Now, as a reward, he began to let himself think about the new condo. He pulled out a pad of graph paper and looked again at the sketch he'd made of its three rooms.

"Jared, you know Orchard Hill at all?" Deanna said.

"Out in Hamden?" he asked thickly. Just getting a sentence out was an effort.

"Uh-huh. That's where they saying that family's at. Remember the one supposed to be sending their kids away?"

It took him a moment. "Oh, yeah. You still on that?"

"Yeah, I just can't— I don't know . . ." She trailed off. "Orchard Hill Road, that *is* Orchard Hill, right?"

Orchard Hill was one of the newer subdivisions, with four-thousand-square-foot houses, triple-bay garages. Not a place DCF usually had occasion to visit. "Yeah, I guess," Jared said, "but that seems like a bit of a stretch. You heard from the school yet?"

"No, not yet. They trying to get permission. To release the records, you know? Oh, wait a minute," she said. "Lane. Orchard Hill *Lane*." She turned back to her computer.

Jared sketched in a couch and a coffee table in a corner of the living room, then thinking better of it, redrew the couch with its back to the open kitchen. Much better. And maybe a couple of chairs?

"Oh *no*!" Deanna groaned.

"What is it?" he said.

She was looking at the computer, reading something. "They went TPR on Porsche," she said.

A bolt of heat flashed through him. "What?" He clicked on his email and saw the one from Will: "Determination, case of Porsche Rivera." He didn't need to read the whole thing, only the one line: ". . . that it is in the best interests of the two boys, as well as the unborn child, to file a petition for termination of parental rights."

He felt his pulse start to race. He'd known she wouldn't be getting her kids back soon, but this was different, this was a move to make it never. Was that what Will had been aiming for all along? Or had Jared's report on the interview been so negative that the committee changed course?

"I mean, I understand he was thinking about the baby, but not to give her one more chance?" Deanna turned to him. She seemed to have shrunk, like an old woman; leathery accordion folds showed around her mouth.

"I-I'm sorry, D," he said. His voice sounded hollow, false.

Deanna didn't seem to notice. "I don't mean you," she said, turning back to the screen. "I know you did the best you could. But sometimes that man is just—*ignorant,* you know? Sitting up there in his fancy house, reading his theories. What does he know about how the rubber hits the road?"

So it was okay, she didn't think it was his fault. Still, his mind seemed to have frozen. He reread the email, not absorbing anything.

"You hungry?" Deanna said after a while.

"It's only eleven."

"I'm thinkin' KFC."

"Serious? Nah, it's too hot."

"They got air-conditioning," she said, "*real* air-conditioning. C'mon. You'll be hungry once you get in that cool air."

—

That evening, as the sun pulsed irritably on the horizon, Jared waited for Eliana in the asphalt-stinking heat of the IKEA parking lot. They were going to check out a couch for the new condo. Check out the couch, grab dinner at that new bistro on the Green, walk back to her place—it was the kind of evening he loved, but for some reason he felt unsettled and he found himself pacing, despite the heat. When he caught sight of Eliana's slim, dark figure walking across the lot, his heart leapt like a fish.

She came up and kissed him. "What's kicking, big guy? How was the day?"

"Same old," he said. "Yours?"

"Good," she said. "Hot, though. I got that new piece started." In the summer, when she wasn't teaching, she worked on her own art. "Fiber work" she called it, not "knitting," as Jared had once made the mistake of saying. The pieces were nice-looking in their strange way; he was looking forward to hanging some in the new condo.

They turned and walked together toward the sliding glass doors, hand in hand. Happy, he'd think later, in sync. So why did he bring up Porsche? There was no reason, really. It was just an itch in him, a wrinkle he wanted smoothed.

"Remember that girl Porsche I told you about?" he said as the doors glided open for them. "They're going TPR on her."

"What's TPR again?" Eliana asked, dropping his hand to untwist the strap of her sleek little Kate Spade backpack.

The backpack and the down payment on the condo and a hundred other luxuries and conveniences were courtesy of her parents back in Philly. The couch, though, he was going to buy himself.

"Termination of parental rights," he said.

She looked up at him, her slender eyebrows arched in surprise. "Termination? Like that's *it,* she'll never get her kids back?"

"Pretty much, yeah."

"Oh God, that's awful!" she said. She actually looked pained.

Jared felt a spasm of annoyance. "She's had many chances, believe me," he said. "And she's blown it every time." This wasn't exactly true—she'd done the rehab, and the parenting course, too, come to think of it—but he wasn't going to complicate things by mentioning all that. "Anyway, we've got to do what's best for the kids."

"Maybe so, but God, forever?" She shook her head. "That's just . . . I don't know."

"Well, she should have thought about that before she screwed up."

Eliana gave him a look. "That's kind of harsh, don't you think? I mean, she didn't choose to screw up."

"Of course she chose," he said. "Sure as hell wasn't anyone *else* choosing." They had reached the base of the escalators. "Furniture's upstairs," he added.

But Eliana had stopped. Her sharp gaze raked his face. "You think people have that kind of control."

"I think they should," he said stubbornly. A part of his own mind looked down at himself in dismay.

"Well then you *do* need to be a lawyer, because you

definitely don't belong in social services," she said. She turned her back on him and stepped onto the escalator.

He put his foot on the jagged edge of the stair behind her. "What the hell does that mean?"

"You want to help people, you got to have *some* compassion."

"I don't have compassion? Two years at the DCF and I don't have compassion? You don't see in a year what I see in a month."

She sliced her eyes away. "It's not a contest, Jared."

"That's not the point."

"Oh yeah? Then what *is* the point?"

They turned to face each other on the landing, something dangerously close to dislike in their eyes. "Forget it," Jared said, quickly, "let's just forget it. It doesn't matter."

She gave him a look but she fell into step beside him, and they wove their way through the displays toward the furniture department, like any other couple on a purchasing mission. Jared knew the couch he wanted: a low, black leather model with a streamlined, 1960s-type shape. He could already picture it bisecting the open living space of their new condo, with a couple of those curved leather chairs on either side.

He located the couch in the third furniture display, set up with a steel-and-glass coffee table and a bright orange rug. "There," he said.

"This is it?" Eliana said.

With a little shock, he noticed that her lower lip was jutting out like a petulant child's. "Yeah," he said, slowly. "You don't like it?"

"Not really."

Jared crossed his arms. "Why? What's wrong with it?"

"I don't know." She shrugged. "It just looks sort of . . . cheap."

"You think that looks cheap," Jared said. "That's a nine-hundred-dollar couch, Eliana. And let me tell you, it's by far the best one in our price range. I know, I checked them all out."

She was not looking at him, had not looked at him, in fact, since they'd stepped off the escalator. What had he done to deserve that? Jared felt his pupils snap in anger. Leaning in toward her, he said the first thing that came into his head. "You have got to get real about our financial situation, Eliana. Unless you want to keep going to your parents for every little thing for the rest of our lives."

He must have raised his voice because two salespeople stopped in the aisle to stare at him—two of them, in a store where finding one was a minor miracle. Jared felt the familiar flush of heat and then, hard on its heels, the old, choking rage. Wasn't he allowed an opinion? Couldn't he express a little aggravation without everyone jumping all over him? No one would have stopped for a white couple arguing, a white man. "We're just discussing a purchase," he called out. "You got a problem with that?"

"No, no, of course not," the saleswoman said, flushing. Then, a beat too late, "Let us know if we can be of assistance!"

"Nosy bitch," he muttered as he turned back.

Eliana's eyes met his: cold, appraising. "It's just a couch, Jared," she said. "You don't have to get all hateful about it."

—

"You hate me, don't you?"

His mother used to say that. Out of the blue, when he thought everything was all right. "You think I'm a pain in the ass, just like your father does.

"It's okay," she would go on calmly, fingering the raggedy end of her brown braid. "I can understand. I don't *like* it, but I can understand it."

She always started out like that: quiet and resigned, like they were talking about something already decided, something no one could do anything about.

"S'not true," Jared would mumble, keeping his eyes on whatever it was he was doing—eating, reading, building one of his models.

Some days that would be the end of it. She would sigh and get up, and after a minute he would calm down enough to go back to whatever he'd been doing. Other times, though, she kept at him. "I just need to know why," she would say. "I mean, what is it that bugs you so much? Is it the way I look? The way I talk? You can tell the truth, Jarey. I can take it," she said, gazing up at the ceiling. "Boy, can I take it." Being hit, she meant. Being hit and getting up again and putting on the tan makeup that she used when his father messed up her face.

And so he would try again: "You don't bug me" or "You're okay. Really." But sometimes it didn't work. She would keep on, piling her words on his sickened and shrinking heart, and after a while they would both be yelling. "Just *tell* me!" his mother would scream. "Tell me the truth!"

"Leave me alone!" he would yell back. By then he did hate her; he did want to hit her. The last time, in fact, he had come close: He had sprung up from his chair and pushed her against the wall, screaming, "Shut up! Shut *up!*"

His father had walked in then and Jared had been strangely relieved to see the clarity and purpose with which he came, the animal gladness of his rage, as he pulled Jared off and knocked him around while his mother screeched "Stop it! Stop it!" from the edge of the room. Afterward, lying on his narrow bed, Jared had let her press the bag of frozen peas to his jaw. She was quiet then, normal—he didn't have to say or do anything. Which was good, because he'd felt a crazy shaking inside, a wild giddiness like the bubbling up of laughter or the first surge of a vicious rage.

—

He and Eliana made up later on her couch, a stained old Pottery Barn sectional her parents had shipped to her when they remodeled their family room.

"I thought you didn't like this couch," she said afterward, licking a drop of sweat off his temple.

"Yeah, well." He was still breathing hard. "It's all right for some things."

"Dog!" she said, but her eyes were laughing.

He put his hand around the back of her head and laid it gently on his chest. He didn't want to joke or even talk. It had come to him suddenly that everything he cared about was wrapped up in that slender, inexpressibly fragile body. He tightened his arms, pressing her like a poultice against his bruised and swollen heart.

—

"I got it!" Deanna called out, waving a piece of paper over her head. "I got it!"

"Got what?" Jared said, turning lethargically. It was only 10:00 a.m. and already the temperature was pushing 100; there was still no sign of the storm system the weatherpeople kept promising. Deanna held the paper out to him. A Care and Protect order, five kids to be removed from their parents' custody, effective immediately. He handed it back. "Which one is this?"

"Orchard Hill Lane, remember? The kids who were disappearing? Looks like the parents been selling them."

"*Selling* them?" he said, doubtfully. "Come on."

"Uh-huh. That's what it looks like anyway. Remember that boy who went to Boston? He told the police up there his mom got five hundred dollars for him. A stack of bills, like in a drug deal or something."

"For real?"

"Looks like it. And they traded another one for a washer and dryer or something, back in the winter."

"Wow," Jared said, "that's—I don't know *what* that is."

She was plowing through some papers on her desk. "Press is gonna be all over this one."

"You going today?"

"Not 'you,' my boy—'we.' We going right now. Grab me a car seat, would you? And a booster? I don't even know how old . . ." Now she was feeling around in her purse. "I guess the police think they're going to sell another one tomorrow. That boy in Boston said . . . Now what did I do—? Oh, here." She fished up a lipstick, and a crumpled tissue flew out.

Jared looked away. That pocketbook of hers was a disaster. And she was getting worse and worse about finishing her sentences. He'd begun to notice things like that, now that he was leaving—little lapses, annoying tics. Immediately, he felt ashamed of himself. He stood up.

Deanna pressed her lips together to spread the lipstick. "You ready? The officers are waiting downstairs."

"Sure," Jared said. He reached behind the file cabinet

to grab a couple of car seats. It was Friday. One more week and he'd be out of there.

—

Jared understood their confusion about the address as soon as they had passed the shopping mall. The road to the Orchard Hill subdivision climbed straight up toward the crest of the hill, where a couple dozen McMansions were scattered across the rolling ground. Orchard Hill Lane turned out to be a side street at the base, directly behind the mall. He and Deanna turned onto it and followed the squad car as it crawled along, looking at numbers. These houses were small and cheaply built, already showing signs of decay: shutters missing, dark gaps around the fascia boards.

After a quarter mile or so, the road came to an abrupt end in a raggedy patch of woods. Through the trees, Jared could just make out the white cinder-block wall of one of the mall's loading docks. A run-down old farmhouse stood on the left, sideways to the street. He glanced over the junk-strewn yard while Deanna struggled to get the car parked. An overturned Big Wheel, a rotting picnic table, some sagging cardboard boxes—DCF territory for sure.

Deanna put the car in reverse to try another pass and irritation spiked in him. "Just leave it," he said sharply. Then, in a softer tone, "You're fine, D."

"You think?" Deanna said, checking her mirrors. "Well, good. You know how I hate parking."

Stepping out into the hot press of the air, they picked their way through the clutter to the front porch, the officers following in the swaggering, wide-legged way they all seemed to share. There was a nasty odor by the stairs, something dead maybe. Jared resisted the urge to hold his nose.

Deanna knocked on the edge of the bent screen door. "Hellooo!" she called.

Like a friend, Jared thought, like someone they might actually want to see.

After what seemed like forever, a skinny white girl came to the door, a cigarette in her mouth. She looked twelve, maybe thirteen at most.

"You must be Melissa," Deanna said. "I'm Deanna Johnson. We spoke on the phone."

The girl took out the cigarette with practiced fingers. "She don't want to talk to you."

"I know, honey, but I got a court order, see?" She gestured behind herself, at the officers. "You're gonna have to let us in, all right?"

The girl's narrowed eyes were the color of sea glass. Their sullen, jaded expression did not change, but she opened the door, stood aside.

The interior of the house was dark and, surprisingly, cool. An effect of the covered porch, Jared thought; those old-time farmers knew what they were doing. He'd have to tell Eliana. It was something they liked to talk about, designing their own house someday.

Deanna was speaking to the girl, telling her what to pack. Jared stepped around an empty TV box to let the officers precede him. He hated going into other people's houses. All of the smells, the animal things that went on—bathroom things, sex things—he didn't want to know about any of that.

The officers had gone into the living room, to the left of the stairs. One of them was talking to a person Jared guessed must be the mother. He walked to the doorway and stopped. She was fairly young, the mother. Like a china doll—alabaster skin, the same sea-glass eyes as the daughter. A china doll going to fat, he amended, noting the bulge of flesh spilling over her jeans.

"That's bullshit," she said to the officer, her face twisting into ugliness. "Fuckin' *bull*shit."

The officer opened his hands in a gesture of helplessness. "Could be, ma'am," he said. "Could well be. I can't be the judge. Like I said, it's only temporary. You can tell your side of things at the hearing. Get it all straightened out."

"Fuckin' *bull*shit," the mother said again.

Now the other officer stepped forward. He was taller and heavier, and his square face had the set, unpleasant look of a snapping turtle's. "We all set here, Al?"

"Just a sec," Al said. He turned back to the woman and put his hands together as if to beg or pray. "It's just for a few days," he said. "Okay?"

The mother reached over and took a cigarette from a flattened pack of Red & Whites.

"We got a court order, ma'am," the bigger officer said. "If you don't surrender the children voluntarily, we're going to have to take them."

She looked up, and Jared saw that her eyes were hard with anger. "So fuckin' take 'em then," she said.

"It's just temporary," Al said. "You can sort it out in court."

"Fuck you," she muttered.

Al shrugged and turned away. In the silence Jared heard Deanna in the hallway, speaking in that cutesy, high-pitched voice she used with young children. "Let's pack up a few of your favorite outfits, okay? You have a favorite T-shirt? Or a favorite toy? . . . Oh, is this your other sister? Hi! I'm Deanna. What's your name?"

The mother was smoking, looking off at nothing.

Deanna leaned in the doorway. "Jared," she said quietly, "would you get the baby?"

He looked where she was pointing. At the corner of the couch, next to the mother's feet, was a baby sleeping in a car seat. He hadn't even noticed it.

The mother looked up at him as he walked over, a blank look, empty even of hostility, and Jared felt a flash of sympathy. "Excuse me," he said, softly. He pointed at the baby. "I just need to—"

In one swift movement she stood up, flung away her cigarette, and scooped the baby into her arms. For a second, everything was still; then the baby's face crumpled into a scream. "You ain't takin' my baby," she snarled.

Deanna and the two officers all started talking at once: they had a court order; there would be a hearing; it was only temporary. Jared barely heard them. A wild alarm was pulsing through him. The mother was in front of him, less than an arm's length away, her eyes watching him with an expression he knew by heart: the cornered, defiant look of a woman who knew she was in for it.

He couldn't help himself; he stepped back.

A gleam came into the mother's eyes; one corner of her mouth turned up in a sneer. "What a big man," she said. "Tryin' to take a baby from her mother."

Jared stared at her, the baby's screams concussing his ears.

"Whatcha gonna do, big man? Huh? You gonna take my baby?"

Later, trying to piece it all together, Jared would wonder why he hadn't thought to just move aside, let the officers do it. There would have been no shame in that. But his brain seemed to have seized.

"I'm gonna get her arm," he heard the big officer say, "then you get the baby, okay?"

The mother kept her gaze on Jared as the cop slowly forced her right arm behind her back. "Big man," she hissed, her eyes bright with derision. "What a big man."

"It's okay, Jared," Deanna said from the doorway. "You just go on."

Jared could feel the officers looking at him. He was acting like a fool, he knew, like a child. He made himself step forward into the glare of the mother's eyes. Blindly, he reached out his hands.

He heard the screech a split second before it hit him. Not the mother—she was still looking right at him—but something that came from the side. Claws raked his skin; then he felt the shock of the teeth, scissoring into his forearm. He flung out his arms and whatever it was flew off him and hit the wall.

For a moment the weird cat screech cut out and the only sound was the baby screaming. Jared had a split second to see his attacker—her spindly little-girl limbs, the flyaway hair—before she was on him again. He raised his arms, threw her off. Out of the corner of his eye he saw Al spin around on the balls of his feet, light as a dancer, and grab her out of the air.

"Jesus, Jared!" Deanna said. "Get *ahold* of yourself!"

He stood there, panting. The kid was yowling and kicking in Al's hairy arms, trying to scratch him, too. Still, Jared could see now that it was just a little girl, no more than six or seven; her contorted face was wet with tears.

He sat down on the couch and put his fist in his mouth.

—

He had to wait while the children's clothes were organized, and the baby soothed, and decisions made about which children would go in which car and where they'd be taken.

Had to wait and not speak—not that anyone would have spoken to him anyway. They moved around him like he wasn't there, like disgrace had made him invisible.

He just needed to get in the car with Deanna, was what he kept thinking—ride back with her, talk to her alone. This was easy enough, as it turned out; no one else offered to take him. But even after they had finally started to drive, he had to keep waiting while the little boy and the baby wailed in the backseat. He kept his eyes fixed straight ahead. The sky had turned an ugly bruised color along the horizon; the storm finally coming, maybe.

"They asleep?" Deanna whispered, after a time.

The crying had stopped, Jared realized. He turned around. The baby's head was lolling; out cold. Even the toddler's eyes were sealed shut; a few tears still clung to the lavender lids. "Yeah," he said.

"Good."

He could hear no animosity in her voice, no judgment. "D, I don't know what happened back there," he began in a rush. "I didn't mean— I don't know. It was just— That wasn't *me* is what I'm trying to say." A part of his brain noted her set face, the fact that she was not looking at him, but he stumbled on. "It was just, I don't know, like an instinct or something. I mean, she came at me like—like some kind of animal, you know? And I just—"

Deanna turned, and he saw that her wide eyes were blazing. "No, that was *you*, Jared," she said. "*You* the animal."

He noted the shock moving through his body as though he were watching it happen to someone else. "*I'm* the animal?" he heard himself say. "She attacked *me*! I was just trying to do what you told me to. You said 'get the baby' and next thing I knew—"

"You threw that child, Jared! Twice! I mean, maybe once, okay, 'cause you were startled or whatever. But twice?" She shook her head. "That was a child, Jared! A *child*!"

There was no escaping the disgust in her voice, the condemnation.

"So that's what you think of me," he said. "That's who you think I really am."

"All I'm saying is that was you did that, Jared. That was *you*."

He looked out the window, unseeing. He knew he hadn't meant any harm; he'd just reacted instinctively, to protect himself. Yet even this certainty seemed to be dissolving. He had hurt that little girl and everyone had seen it. A gray tide of despair rose in him.

Deanna turned onto Dixwell Avenue. Newhallville. Jared gazed bitterly at the cheap little frame houses, the trash-strewn lots. People were sitting together on some of the porches, waiting for the storm, their dark skin bright with sweat. Once Jared had looked at such scenes with hunger and envy; then, later, in the fullness of his happiness with Eliana, his confidence about the future, he had ceased even to notice them. And now? What now? For it had come to him suddenly that he would have to tell Eliana. And when he told her, when she added this to the scene he'd made in IKEA, to the little she knew about his father—what then? In his mind's eye, the future turned to ash.

Suddenly, Deanna slammed on the brakes and he was thrown forward.

"Jesus Lord!" she cried. Figures were flashing past the front of the hood. The van to their left fishtailed, brakes squealing, and Jared saw the three boys clearly; they were running toward the middle of the road. Young kids, barely into double digits. What Porsche's sons would be in a few short years.

"Jesus Lord!" Deanna said again, checking the rearview mirror to see if the children had woken up, her foot still on the brake. The van driver hadn't moved either; he was rolling down his window, yelling something at the boys, who had stopped together on the double yellow line.

They were dressed convict-style, Jared noticed, in sagging pants and overlarge T-shirts. Well, that was the future they were probably heading for anyway, he thought, grimly. Because really, what were their chances? But oh, how bright they looked, how alive, as they laughed and called out to each other and bumped each other's knuckles—how young and lithe and full of promise.

Like he had been.

A feeling rose in Jared's throat, hard and raw and lumped as a fist. He glanced over at the traffic on the other side of the street. The cars were coming fast and way too close together; surely the boys would stay put. But no—they were leaning forward, they were getting ready to run.

He watched, his breath balled in the back of his mouth, as they sprang into the road.

THREE VIEWS
OF A POND

I

She saw it in her mind's eye: the sunken round of ice, the sloping white bank. There was no need to think of a method, no need to plan. She had said, "I will kill myself," and immediately she saw it: the pond and the bridge, the black gap by the dam where the ice didn't form.

All these weeks, as she walked across campus, as she sat in the dining hall—measuring the trickle of skim milk into her coffee, eating half portions of salad—all this time some secret part of her had been scouting the landscape like a hungry animal, keen with purpose. She had decided this—she.

An image came to her of her mother, holding her as a baby. It was a photo from the family album and inside its old-fashioned, scalloped edges her mother was young and smiling, her new baby wrapped tight in a blanket on her lap. A sweet, faultless little baby; a tiny girl. A sob swelled her throat. But it was too late, she had already decided. She stared in horror at the sun-filled quad outside her dorm room window. The shoveled paths, the bright face of the building across the way, even the light itself seemed to have turned away from her. A handful of birds flung up into the blue air and scattered.

"Okay," she whispered.

It had begun with her body. Or perhaps it hadn't, she couldn't quite remember, but it was in her body that she felt it. Her body was wrong, it was queer and crooked, misshapen in a thousand ways. She couldn't keep track of them all, even looking in the mirror she couldn't exactly tell. Sometimes she thought it was her hips (grotesquely curved) or her shoulders (huge like a man's) or her full, almost gluttonous lips. Often, though, it was nothing she could pinpoint, it was just the instant sinking of her heart: She saw herself and she saw that she was wrong.

She could feel it as she walked to class or in the dining hall when she stood in line with the normal, small, pretty girls. Even when she tried to joke there was a hideous undercurrent to her words, a darkness she saw reflected in the faces of those around her. (What was it Ana had said? "You are never seeming happy.")

She had tried to change. She made rules: no speaking unless spoken to; no negative comments; no more than two thousand calories a day. These were reasonable rules, limits normal people followed instinctively, but she broke them again and again. Her days were a series of battles. Getting dressed took a wrenching hour; even going to breakfast was an ordeal, a maze of choices she could not make. (Should she eat? And who could she sit with? And if she did, what would she say?) Moments of clarity were worse. Terrible truths came to her then, truths which, because they came calmly, were irrefutable. *They don't like you.* Or, *You will fail.* Or, *You will kill yourself.* She was a black hole, a howling core of darkness, and she couldn't hide it. At the library, for instance, when she had seen the young reference librarian laughing with a short-haired girl in the warm light of the desk lamp. She could have passed by; instead she'd walked over to them. She had a question—it was normal to have a question, she told herself—but when she began to speak, she saw the laughter slide off the librarian's face.

"Yes?" the woman said, her expression suddenly terrible, like a mask.

"Criticism," she blurted.

"Excuse me?"

"Um, criticism—for Frost?" she stumbled. It was not even a real question. She felt her face begin to burn. The other girl dropped her eyes.

"I would recommend you look in the card catalog," the librarian said, "under 'F.'"

Walking away, she'd heard a short, snorting laugh behind her. Or had she? It was a sound so precisely like her nightmares, she doubted it was real.

She stood, now, at the window of her dorm room, her

hands on her face. She could feel her fingers cradling her cheeks and her slack mouth and through her mouth the breath coming, shallow and quick. Two girls were walking down one of the paths in the quad, laughing. Their legs moved them toward each other and away, toward and away, as though they were connected by elastics.

She, too, had walked down that path earlier. She looked back at herself across the vast distance of the day: a tiny, innocent figure walking to her Renaissance Drama class. Nothing had happened yet; it was just a morning, with the sun shining weakly through a lifting fog. Then, by the library, a young man in a ridiculous wool hat had turned and smiled at her. He leaned out and slipped something into the palm of her glove.

"Look at it," he said, his voice sudden and close.

She had not intended to stop but as she brushed past him she felt her hair catch in the stubble on his face and she turned, startled, to see his blue eyes looking straight into hers. Something had leapt up in her then, frantic as a dog, and she had walked away quickly, the flyer creasing in her hand.

"Tonight! The Iron Horse!" he'd called behind her. "Think about it!"

She had a queasy feeling in her belly, as of two antithetical elements poisonously mixing. When the gray stone classroom building loomed before her, she turned off on a path that led back behind the library. She did not think or reason with herself, she simply went, weaving her way through the buildings back to her dorm room, where, with her door shut on the deserted hall, she took out the scissors and cut her hair to the scalp.

That was why she'd been bald when Ana came to her door, bald with the blood just drying where the scissors had scraped, and her eyes still red from crying.

"But, Leila," Ana exclaimed, "you have cut all your hair!"

The sound of her own name seemed to strike her like a slap. She had opened the door on impulse, without even glancing in the mirror, for the knock had sounded somehow like a reprieve. But now she felt Ana's eyes on her, sharp as a sparrow's, and she realized how she must look.

"It is very short!" Ana said brightly, in her pretty Mexican accent.

She nodded.

"Maybe that is a fashion now?" Ana herself was wearing pressed khakis and a pink oxford shirt.

"Maybe," she said grimly.

Ana looked down at the hall floor. "Well. I'm sure it will be . . . it will be looking very good." She looked up again with a little toss of her head; her black hair swung out and back in its smooth, thick curve. She had come to invite her to a party. "A salsa party," she said. "We will be having a piñata. Do you know what is a piñata?"

Leila did not answer. She could feel herself disappearing under the bright rain of Ana's words. A slow fury began to heat in her chest.

"Well, it is very much fun," Ana was saying. "It is an animal or even a star or something like that and it is of colored paper, very beautiful, and inside there is candy. So you take sticks and—you have a napkin around your eyes like this, you know?—and you take sticks and try to hit it. It is very fun. You will have to—"

"No," she said, looking straight at Ana through her monstrous red eyes.

"I'm sorry?"

"I'm not coming."

A flash of something hard passed across Ana's face. "I just thought it would make you feel happy, Leila," she said. She folded her arms across her chest. "Because you are never seeming happy. You are never seeming happy and I wonder even do you want—"

She shut the door so abruptly Ana had to step backward, and for a moment, as she leaned there with the knob pressing into her belly, she felt a wild urge to laugh. But then she saw what she had done.

She thought of it now without emotion, this interaction that had convinced her to kill herself. The crying, the cutting, the frenzy were all over. None of it mattered now. Outside, the two girls had disappeared; the paths were empty. As she watched, the birds settled on the snow near the steps and began pecking warily at the broken pieces of bread scattered there.

After a time she realized that she was no longer thinking—her mind had fallen open like a hand worn out from gripping. She turned from the window and lay down, fully clothed, on the narrow bed.

When she woke it was dark and her belly was sour and hollow. Hungry, she realized, and why not? She put on a baseball hat and slowly opened her door; the hall was clear. She went to the bathroom to wash her swollen face.

The night air was cold. She felt it on her damp skin: the shock of it and then the fading of the shock as she walked, placing her feet with care on the icy path. There was no need to think, no need to worry. At the dining hall, she took a piece of fried chicken with her salad; the serving woman smiled at her. The vast room was deserted. It was Friday, she remembered; there was a French theme dinner at another hall.

She ate by herself in a small pool of quiet by the window. The wooden chairs, the smell of hot food, the round, solid table surface filled her with relief. She felt sleepy and cleansed, like a child after a tantrum.

You will have to get up very early so no one will see you, she thought. Her implacable, unappeasable mind.

But there was no need to think of that yet. She stuck her hand out and hid the bloody string of the drumstick under her napkin. Outside, the sky was turning an electric blue. Later it would be black and she would see the stars, pinpricks of light in the dark flat of her window.

II

The pond was nearly invisible in the darkness, save for a gleam here and there where the light from the lamppost hit it. The noise of it, however, was all around her—splashing and rushing and burbling, a chorus of secret murmurings. It felt overstated, like her own presence there. She didn't belong on campus anymore—she'd graduated the spring before—and yet she'd agreed to come back, for a dance in the old college boathouse on the other side of the pond. Or no, not agreed—proposed it herself. *A mistake*, she thought now.

She stopped at the center of the bridge, where the circle of light from the last lamppost faded out. Behind her, she heard Alexa stop as well. There was the pop of a match being lit and then the greedy noise of the flame biting into the tobacco. She turned to see Alexa flick the match over the railing, a spark swallowed by darkness.

"Is that it?" Alexa said, nodding toward the lights of the boathouse.

"Yeah," she said. The sounds of the dance were clearly audible now: the thud-thud of the bass; high, ragged snatches of shouting. It was a women's dance, put on by the college women's center. She couldn't imagine now why she'd ever thought of going, let alone inviting Alexa.

"Want one?" Alexa said, holding out her pack of cigarettes.

"No thanks. I don't smoke."

"Smart."

Leila leaned against the railing for support, overcome by the odd weakness that had dogged her all evening, and arranged her arms into what she hoped was a relaxed position. At the restaurant she and Alexa had talked easily enough, but as soon as they'd stepped out into the darkness, they'd fallen silent, and now it seemed that nothing could be said, nothing except what didn't matter. She looked down at Alexa's shoes, which were thick-soled and bulky, with a stripe of fake leopard. They were the first thing she'd noticed when she came through the restaurant door: those odd shoes and the too-big leather jacket and the strange way Alexa was leaning against the hostess station, as though she'd been waiting for hours and all hope had left her. And yet when Alexa had looked up, she'd noticed her startling, gray-green eyes and then, walking to the table, her slim figure weaving ahead through the chairs. There was some quality attached to her, a kind of heat or light, as though her body left an afterimage in the air.

Alexa took a drag and exhaled. "So you're really not a smoker."

She shook her head.

"Smart," Alexa said again. She stood, curved-shouldered, in the center of the bridge, cradling the elbow of her smoking arm in her other hand.

"I just never wanted to for some reason," Leila said. "I don't know."

"Very smart." Alexa took another drag.

She waited for Alexa to say something more, but she didn't; she had turned her back and was staring off in the direction of the boathouse. The water falling over the dam was making the same series of sounds over and over, like a skip on a record. That was all, then, she thought, nothing would happen. Still, something in her couldn't bear to give up. She thought of Alexa at dinner, stretching her hand out to show the tiny bump in the hollow between her fingers. The doctor had said it was nothing, just a cyst, but Alexa seemed to take no comfort in that.

"Before it was in my neck," she said in a low voice, leaning across the table. "It's traveling all over my goddamn body!"

Leila looked into Alexa's panicked eyes and then, for some reason, burst out laughing.

"You're laughing? I've got a goddamn tumor traveling around my body and you're laughing?"

"It's a cyst!" she managed to say.

"Yeah, but it could turn *into* cancer. I could still die." The start of a smile bent one corner of Alexa's mouth.

"Yeah, and you could get hit by a bus, too," she said, laughing harder. "Right? Splat, the end."

With Alexa she had always had these unexpected moments of strength. They had met when Alexa came to campus to teach a video class during Leila's last semester. On the first day of spring shopping week, Alexa had stood in front of the classroom, her hands on her hips, barking out the class requirements. She was short and small-boned, but the way she stood, with her feet planted and her weight back, gave an impression of power. Students were sitting on the radiators and standing up inside the open doorway, mostly lesbians and women's studies majors. A video of Alexa's had been shown a few days before and word had gotten out. Leila was careful not to ask herself what she was doing there.

"This is not a course for people who just want to screw around a little," Alexa said, running her light, impassive eyes over the crowd. "If you're not serious, you don't belong here."

A girl with short purple hair raised her hand.

"Yes."

"What if you want to screw around a *lot*?"

A few people laughed but Alexa's face remained expressionless. "That's your prerogative," she said. "Just don't do it in here. Next?"

In the end, there had to be a lottery. The only reason Leila made it in was because seniors were given priority. She sat in the back and avoided asking questions. She had less experience than most of the other students and didn't want to draw attention to herself. Also, she had a vague sense that Alexa might turn out to be an adversary. There were certain incidents that seemed to confirm this: an angry look when she was late to class one day; a time when Alexa called on her ("You, in the back") and then waited, arms crossed, while she stumbled through her answer.

Then one afternoon Leila had come in after hours to

return a camera and found Alexa kicking furiously at a tangle of tripods on the floor.

Alexa looked up. Her face had a disarranged look, like a hastily made bed.

"I was just bringing the camera—"

"Sure, okay. Over there." Alexa jerked her chin toward the table at the end of the room.

"Thanks." Leila crossed the room as quickly as she could. She put the camera on the table and was turning to go when she realized she'd forgotten to sign the clipboard. Flushing, she scribbled the time and date under the "return" column and signed her name. When she looked up, she saw that Alexa wasn't even watching, she was leaning against the wall with one arm wrapped around herself and a hand over her eyes.

Leila hesitated. Whatever was going on had nothing to do with her, and yet the sight of Alexa's small, hurt back seemed to pierce her. She went over and knelt down before the pile of tripods and began to gently tug the legs free. It wasn't such a mess, really; it only took a few minutes. Alexa was still leaning against the wall, her face hidden, when Leila left.

A week or so later, she came late to class again, sweating from her run across the campus. Feeling Alexa's eyes on her as she pulled the door shut, she steeled herself. But when she glanced up, she saw that it wasn't a look of reproof; it was more like the kind of long, absorbed gaze you might cast over a lake.

She sat down quickly, confused. *It couldn't be*, she thought, but she was suddenly conscious of the sweep of her own body—her neck, the scoop of bare skin above her breasts. Alexa was writing a list of required shots on the board. Leila opened her notebook and wrote the date on the top of the first empty page. Bird chatter and the cold smell of damp earth were coming through the window. Spring. With careful strokes, she began to copy the list of shots into her notebook.

That had been the beginning of a season colored and bent by longing. There were little interactions flushed with promise—a moment rigging up cables together, a joke that made Alexa laugh; once, near the end of the semester, an awkward excursion for coffee. But they hadn't said anything; whatever it was between them, if there was anything, remained unspoken, and Alexa had gone back to New York. It had ended the way such things always ended for Leila, without ever really happening.

Suddenly, there was a surge of music from the boathouse. "You're crazy!" someone yelled. "You're all crazy!" Laughter and the thunk of the old wooden door shutting. They watched a figure stumble toward the bridge. It was a girl, dressed in the jeans and plaid shirt that were the unofficial uniform of the lesbians on campus.

Alexa stepped back and leaned against the railing next to her. "Incoming," she said softly.

The girl looked at them as she went by, her upturned face

moony in the dim light. "They'rrrrall *crazzy,*" she breathed at them.

Neither of them answered. They were not being malicious, it was just that she had nothing to do with them or with the feeling that had suddenly sprung up between them. A kind of symmetry, it felt like, an invisible lining up, involuntary as the movement of the needle hands on a compass.

The girl put her head down and charged unsteadily toward the other end of the bridge. They watched her disappear into the shadow of the woods.

"*She* must've had some fun," Alexa said.

"Mmmm," Leila said. For a moment they stayed there, parallel.

Then Alexa threw her cigarette away and turned to face her. "So, what do you say—should we go to this thing?" There was something guarded in her eyes, a flatness that was almost hostile.

Leila looked away, as one might with a nervous dog. "I think we should do whatever we want," she said carefully. "I mean, what the hell." She glanced back. "Tomorrow we could get hit by a bus."

Alexa laughed. "True."

They both looked off, at the murky darkness that was the pond.

"What do *you* want?" Alexa said, very close.

She looked into Alexa's eyes looking into hers. There was

a humming in her ears. "I don't know," she mumbled. But she did, of course; she had known all along.

"Leila," Alexa whispered, and the sound of her name was like a cord pulled through the center of her. Everything that was wrong, all that was blackened and torn and shameful, fell away.

III

"Have you seen it?" Mara asked.

"No," Leila said. They were sitting in a grassy area beside the pond in the bright spring sunlight, painting their toenails. Leila and Susan were visiting; Mara still lived there, in a spooky old Victorian a few blocks away. The nail polish had been Mara's idea. It was the kind of impulse they liked to indulge on these rare weekends together. The frivolity, the sheer purposelessness of it gave them a taste of that time before plans and obligations had hemmed them in—those lost, sunny afternoons when the hours arced out, suspended, like a high-flung ball.

"You really should, Leila," Susan said, examining her from under the visor of her upheld hand. "I think it's the best movie I've seen all year."

"I'd love to," Leila said.

Susan looked back down at her toes and Leila felt a trace of relief. That was something she had learned from them, that tone of affirmation. They spoke like that, they said "I'd love to" or "She's amazing" or "This is delicious." None of it was false, they meant what they said; it was a bias they had, an instinct for the positive, just as she, in the past, had leaned toward the negative. So now she had learned. She said, "I'd love to"; she kept her foot in the ring. Although the truth was, she couldn't care less if she saw that movie; she couldn't care less if she saw any movie, ever again.

She looked out across the glassy surface of the pond. On the banks here and there people were sunning, their skin showing greenish white where they had rolled back their clothes. Spring had come again, with its flowers and bugs, its painful, vivid beauty. She seemed to be noticing it with a peculiar intensity this time: the shiny, unfurling leaves; the birds frantically nesting. She felt the miracle of it and at the same time the wasting to come (a crow would steal the eggs; the leaves would dull and wither), so that even an ordinary sight, like the bright green pollen lying squandered on the pond, cut her to the quick.

Susan tipped her foot to see the polish sparkle. "Nice color!" she said in a fake Brooklyn accent. "What's it called?"

"Love Her Madly," Mara said, "and let me tell you, this shit is *hot*."

They laughed. Leila smiled, so as not to seem left out. They had come to comfort her, ditching their men for the holiday weekend because they knew she was in trouble. She could feel their concern, the push and tug of it, like an invisible net around her, and was grateful. But it was not a net that could hold, she knew. Nothing could hold a person once she began to fall, nothing external, anyway.

They had been coming to this pond ever since they graduated, she and Mara and Susan, because it was green and nearby, because they had come the year before. For a long time these visits had found them more or less unchanged. A lover would have vanished or a new job been taken, but they were still safely the same, still in that long, slow glide of young adulthood. Now it was finally ending. There had been signs for a while: wrinkles setting in, a gray hair or two, the looming biological milestone of thirty-five. But now they really had turned the corner. Susan was pregnant, Mara was getting married, and Leila and Alexa were splitting up.

She pictured the kitchen at home as it must look now, the cupboards pulled open and pillaged, the stacks of boxes labeled in Alexa's neat hand. She and Alexa would not own a farm in France or travel to Mongolia. They would not adopt a child or raise their own goats or any of the other things they had dreamed up over the years; they would not be together.

"You could use a justice of the peace," Susan was saying.

"That's true," Mara said. "I wonder about Derek's mom, though, you know? You should put on a second coat, by the way," she added, squinting at Susan's toes.

"Really? Okay. Why his mom? Is she religious?"

"Well, yes and no—actually, I can't say that. I don't really know. I just get the feeling that, you know, she wouldn't like it."

"Yeah, but Mar, this is *your* wedding, not hers."

"True," Mara said.

They were silent and Leila heard the sound of the water spilling over the dam at the end of the pond. Ruthless, it seemed to her, excessive, like someone dumping pitcher after pitcher of water onto the ground. *Better than listening to them blather about weddings,* she thought, and then: *How awful.* She was awful, with her dry, bitter seed of a heart.

"What about your dress?" Susan said.

"Well, that's another issue." Mara lifted her small, pretty foot and picked something off one of the nails.

Leila looked down at her own feet. The skin on the heels was a strange, translucent yellow. She had begun to be haunted again by the specter of her body, its disturbing particularity. That sense of grace, the secret loveliness she had found in the gray expanse of Alexa's eyes had been snuffed out. Alexa no longer loved her; she had fallen in love with someone else.

A shadow fell over her. It was a man in a plaid shirt, bending low to hold the hand of a little girl clad in nothing but a diaper; her small, bowed legs moved with stubborn purpose toward the water. The man shrugged his shoulders in their direction as he walked, crablike, in her wake.

"She looks like she knows what she wants," Susan called out.

"You better believe it," he said. He was a young man, although balding; younger than they were, maybe.

Susan turned to Mara. "So cute!" she said.

"Totally." They watched the little girl with a pleased, almost proprietary air.

"So you think sleeveless is okay?" Mara asked after a minute.

"Absolutely! I mean, why not?" Susan said. "Show off those arms."

"Good," she sighed.

They would do that, Susan and Mara, they would go on to live in the happy chaos of marriage and children, that sunny carnival that went on and on—daycare and homework and college and grandchildren—until you were safe in the grave. *One flesh*, Leila thought. It really was like that. She and Alexa had slept back to back with the soles of their feet pressed together. Even after they fought, even when they were furious they had done that, their feet traveling to find each other under the cover of sleep.

She gazed, stunned, at the suddenly desolate landscape. A cloud had blotted out the sun, the pond had turned dull as lead. Mara's dress, Susan's baby, the green buds beading the bushes—what did it matter? The future stretched out before her like a desert. Even the afternoon, even the next ten minutes and the ten that would follow, seemed as merciless, as measured as a punishment. She would have to sit there while Mara and Susan finished their nails; then there would be the walk back, slow, to accommodate Susan, then the dinner to wait through, and the whole evening and night and morning before she could get in her car and go. And then?

Abruptly, she stood.

"You okay?" Mara said.

Leila gestured vaguely toward the open grass, not looking at them. "Walk," she muttered.

"Okay," Mara said gently.

She stumbled off with their eyes on her back. Ridiculous to take off like that, rude, even, but she couldn't sit there another second. She walked twenty paces, unseeing, and was brought up short by the cement edge of the dam. Anguish clutched her, hard as a fist.

Then she saw: It was Alexa's feet—her feet and eyes and laugh and soft, freckled belly—all of it, everything she would never have again. Her eyes filled with tears. She sat down by the dam and waited, rabbit-hunched, for the pain to ebb.

Years ago, when she was in college, she had planned to kill herself in this pond. But at the last moment things had come up—she'd overslept; a girl from the next hall invited her sledding; she'd seen a cardinal, red as a heart, in the leafless tangle of a bush. This and that small thing had happened—time had passed—and the terrible gap had closed.

She had thought of it again in April, when she finally understood that Alexa was leaving. They were sitting on the kitchen floor with their backs against the cabinets, like squatters in an abandoned house, although the table and chairs were right in front of them. They had decided already or at least the words had been spoken—hard, definite words that she had uttered and understood with one clear corner of her brain.

"What are you going to do?" Alexa had asked. "Will you get a roommate?"

She was sitting next to Leila and her eyes were the same eyes, the hair on her arms the same hair that Leila had held the rights to for so many years, yet to touch her now would have been a gross violation, an ugliness.

I could kill myself, Leila had thought.

But she wasn't going to; she knew that, although she couldn't have said why, what was different this time. She watched a swallow dip low over the water and then, with a flick of its wings, sweep sideways. She had been wrong, all those years ago, about the gap in the ice. It hadn't been in the pond, it had been on the other side of the dam, where the water rushed onto the rocks and away. She'd noticed it a few days later when she was out for a jog.

"Here comes the sun!"

That was Susan, calling out. Leila turned, and as if on cue, the pond lit up and she saw the tiny, golden insects moving frantically above the water. She looked back at her friends from across the span of grass. They were both watching the pond: Mara, absorbed, a smile of wonder curving her mouth; Susan, still worried, her forehead wrinkled.

Leila breathed in. It was true that she might never find

another partner; also that she might not have children. That was how it was, she thought, looking at the pollen scattered on the pond's surface—some made it, some were cast aside. And all the time it went on: the sky, the water, the greening trees; the endless kaleidoscope of the world, breaking and joining, breaking and joining.

She watched the swallow labor up into the brilliant sky. In the morning, she would drive back to the apartment. She would buy some flowers, start again. It was possible things wouldn't get better, but it was also possible they would.

Susan and Mara were talking about the baby now, about names. Leila turned her head to watch the glassy curve of water sliding over the dam, smooth and pliant as a muscle. She could see the coiled force of it, the relentless pull inside the curl. But the pond itself looked still, the trees and underbrush reflected as perfectly as in a mirror. If it hadn't been for the pollen, she wouldn't have even known it was moving.

ANIMALS

We killed the porcupines because they were sneaking into the barn at night and chewing on the floor beams. My father walked right up to them and shot them through their little eyes.

"That's the only way to get at them," my mother said, "their skulls are so thick."

I saw them the next morning, stacked in the wheelbarrow by the driveway—two big ones and two little ones. My father was going to dump them in the ditch up the road.

My friend Amy buried dead animals in her backyard in town. She had a little red wagon and some rubber gloves her mother gave her and she would walk out to Route 112 to pick up any animal that was killed there. She let me help her one day when I stayed after school to play. She had a dead squirrel from the day before, laid out in tissue paper inside a yellow shoe box. We dug a hole by the fence in the backyard and put the box inside. Lisa taped two sticks together to make a cross and stuck it in the dirt we put on top. There was a whole row of little crosses, just like in a cemetery.

I told my parents about it when I got home.

My father put down his knife and pushed back his plate. "That sort of nonsense is okay for a city kid," he said.

We killed the beavers because they were ruining the north field. They were building a dam in a long loop across the stream; every day the water spread out a little more behind it. My father went and broke the dam in the evenings, but by the morning it was always put back together again, so he got some dynamite and blew it up. Then he and Hop Johnson set traps along the stream bank so they could catch the beavers when they came out to rebuild.

The deer were so my father could relax with his buddies when the farmwork wound down in the fall. The rabbits were for the same reason, but also to give his beagle, Jake, a run and not the kind of run he had when he got loose and took off with Pogo, because Pogo was a mutt and would give chase to anything. "That mutt's got no place on a farm," my father said.

On a farm, the animals come first. Feed the animals before you feed yourself, my mother always said—you can wait, they can't. Feed them first and always feed at the same time, otherwise the horses will pick on each other and the cows will get into mischief and hurt themselves. In the mornings, you don't want to feed the animals. You would rather do anything than open the covers and stick your legs out into the biting air, but your mother said to, so you do. You put on your thick peacoat and your heavy rubber boots and you stumble across the rough surface of the field. When you open the barn door, the dumb heat of them greets you through the darkness—the clouds from their nostrils, the sweet smell of their skins. The horses make a welcoming noise. They were waiting for you, and now you've come.

We had to poison the mice or the next thing you knew we'd have rats. The poison came in a yellow box shaped like a cheese wedge. It tasted good to them but when they ate it, it made them bleed inside. In the mornings I would find them drowned in the toilet or lying near the tiny circle of water around the sink drain, their triangular mouths gaping.

With the groundhogs it was the vegetables in the garden. There was no arguing about the damage; I could see it for myself: three rows of chewed green stubs and every few feet the two perfect leaves of a plant they had missed. My dad sat out with the shotgun and waited for them, but they were wily and hard to get, so one Saturday my parents found their holes and plugged them all but one. Then they backed the truck up to it and ran a thick hose from the exhaust pipe down into the opening. My little sister and I stood by with plastic feed bags to stuff in afterward so the good air wouldn't slip in there and save them. That way we got the whole family, my mother said. I was worried that they weren't all in there. What if one of them came back and found everyone dead?

Afterward I called Pogo upstairs to lie on my bed. Cows and chickens and pigs like anyone who feeds them, but a dog is for you alone. You smooth back her ears and stare into the bewildered yellow mirrors of her eyes. She looks back at you from her secret animal face. At night she sleeps in the V of your legs; in the day you abandon her, at least once every day, but she waits for you anyway, and when you come back she is wild with joy. You hold her ears and stare into her eyes and after a minute she jumps up and licks you, licking and wagging and giving you a soft little nip or two so you'll cut out whatever it is you're doing, looking at her that way.

The chickens went to their deaths with their big, musty bodies tucked under my mother's arm. She would walk slowly around the pen at first, as if she were only getting their feed ready, the chickens moving away from her at the same pace, but hopping a little, their eyes jerking. When she grabbed the one she was looking for, the others would squawk and scurry off to the edges of the pen. But by the time she'd wrung its neck they would all be eating again.

When you pluck a chicken you have to touch every pore. It makes you sick—the pull of the skin coming up with the feather and then, when you think you're done, those last wretched spines sticking between the legs. It makes you think of the eggs your class tried to hatch at school, when the boys turned the incubator too high and killed them. Afterward the teacher cut one of them open and called everyone around to see and what you saw was a tiny fetus stuck in the yellow-green of a cooked yolk, exactly like the one you loved to pick out of a hard-boiled egg.

You hand the chicken to your mother in disgust. You won't eat it, not this time. She gives you a look of disbelief so you swear to God. You watch, you say.

In the evening, the crisp, buttery smell of it steals up the stairs while you're doing your homework. The oven turns the bruised yellow skin to gold, and when your father touches it with the knife, juice sparkles up. He carves white feathers of breast meat, golden strips of skin. You eat cold peas and mashed potatoes without gravy under your mother's exasperated gaze. For a week afterward you long for chicken: the tender heat of it, the sweet, folded limbs.

The pig died when the leaves turned red. A different pig each year, but only one. In the spring he was trim and adorable and he bounced up to the fence whenever you passed. But by fall he was fat, dulled and bloated by loneliness. He lay all day at the edge of the pen like the pupil of a crazy eye, and you didn't care if he died, you wanted him to die, you wanted him out of there so the mud would turn to grass again and the wire gate could slump against the fence, an idle curl of mesh.

"Some animals are stupid anyway," I told Amy. "Chickens and cows and pigs are all stupid."

"That's not true," she said. "Pigs are smart. I read a book about it."

"I know that book," I said. "That's a make-believe book."

"No it's not," she said.

"Yes it is," I said, "and if you don't believe me, you can't come to my farm anymore."

With the mowing it wasn't our fault. We had to kill the rabbits and snakes and frogs that jumped up in front of the blade because there wasn't time to yell for the tractor to brake and if we did, the blade might jam and jump off its guide and then our father would have to stop and get down and slam it back into place with the hammer.

If you tried not to notice, you could pretend it wasn't happening. The animals leapt up into the shuddering grass and fell away so fast they might never have been there at all. But every so often you'd see a frog with a missing leg by the edge of the pond, lopsided and terrified, struggling frantically to propel his body to safety.

That was what you saw when Pogo caught the baby groundhog: the groundhog scrambling for the mouth of its burrow and then the white snarl of Pogo's teeth, jerking it back. She shook it like she'd shake a stick you'd thrown her. She tossed it up and caught it; she dropped it and stood over it, waiting for it to move so she could pounce on it again, her ears cocked, her body tense and bright with gladness.

You could see where the whiskers stuck out of the groundhog's nose, its hairless gray belly. When she threw it in the air its mouth opened, and you heard the tiny sound that came out. It was funny almost: the jerk of the body, the mouth flying open. Its fat head went back and forth, back and forth, and something inside you snapped loose, floated up in your throat. Your limbs went slack and ticklish and you burst into a run, leaping across the sunlit grass, yelling,

"Pogo! Pogo!" jumping up and down in front of her. She dropped the groundhog and sprang back, waiting for you to throw it—and then you swung your foot out and kicked her in the ribs.

You stood in the blank rectangle of the field and watched her run from you, the lifeless groundhog in a heap at your feet. At the road, she stopped and looked back. Then she turned away and trotted up the hill into the dark, spread hand of the wood.

—

"Funny she should take off like that," your father says at dinner.

Your mother reaches for the biscuits. "Nothing to do but wait," she says. "She'll come home when she's hungry enough."

You poke at the food on your plate, thinking of the foundation in the woods that your father showed you last fall, a deep, stone-lined square in the ground. He held your jacket while you leaned in to look at the dead German shepherd stretched out in the corner. He had a thin red collar and he lay on his side, as though he were only napping.

"No one would have heard him way up here," your father told you, and then you saw how he must have barked. When he realized he was trapped, he must have barked for someone, and he must have gone on barking and barking up at the trees, but there was no one to hear him and he lay down to wait and he died.

When your parents aren't looking, you take the meat off your plate and stuff it into your napkin. You put it in the dog dish and you put the dish at the end of the porch, where Pogo might smell it and come home. In the morning you wake to the still-empty bed.

"When is Pogo coming back?" your sister asks at breakfast.

"Hopefully soon," your mother says. "Now eat up that oatmeal."

Your sister is still small. She has short legs and blond hair and a tender roll of fat above each wrist. Every day before you leave, your mother kneels down to button her coat for her, the little red coat that used to be yours. You walk her to the school bus alone, the empty rope of your heart bumping along behind you.

All day, the pit of fear grows in your chest and by afternoon you can't wait to get home. You jump off the bus and run to open the front door, hoping for the click of her nails, the thump of her tail against the kitchen cabinets. But the house is empty. You walk back through the rooms like a ghost or a stranger. The blue chair, the broken clock—everything familiar is lost to you.

After your chores, you fill your pockets with scraps of bologna and walk up the hill to the edge of the woods. The cold trees stretch back like stones into the darkness, one behind the other.

"Pogo!" you shout. Your puny voice trails off. In the silence, you hear the red animal of your own heart, pumping blindly in your chest. You turn and run.

In the end, someone finds her. You hear the phone ring and the happy tone of your mother's voice and then she comes into the kitchen smiling at you and you run for the leash and tear across the lawn to jump in the truck after your father, everything good again, the hills in their rightful place, the woods friendly, you and your father speeding over the bumps and hollows of the road, a woodsy, comfortable smell rising from the stiff folds of his hunting jacket.

—

Sometimes we had to kill an animal to stop it from suffering. Like the groundhog in the road—when we saw it up ahead, turning crookedly in a puddle of blood, my mother said, "Stop the car. It's not fair to let a creature suffer like that."

She got out and took a stone off the wall that ran along the road and dropped it on the groundhog's head. The animal lurched forward and then jerked back a little, as if a great, clumsy spring were recoiling inside it. When it was completely still, she kicked it slowly into the weeds.

It was the same thing with Pogo's puppy. It had been made wrong in Pogo's womb and its lungs didn't work. It lay on its side at the edge of the box, its tiny pink mouth grabbing at the air.

"We're going to have to put that puppy out of its misery," my mother said. But my sister and I thought it might get better, so she left us there for a while to watch it choke, its great, blind head tipped sideways.

"Can't we call the doctor?" my sister whispered. She was rolling her hands in her shirt so that her little belly stuck out.

"Shhh," I said. I was watching for a change in its breathing. It would have to breathe and then it would have to nurse like the others. Once or twice, I thought it was getting better, but when my mother came back, I could see that it hadn't really changed.

"We've got two choices," my mother said. "We can suffocate it in a bag or we can drown it."

My sister and I sat there looking at it. It had two perfect ears and a white stripe on its nose. "Suffocate?" my sister said. But my mother said drowning would be faster. She picked the puppy up. Pogo jumped out of the box and followed us, but she kept looking back at the rest of the litter and after a minute she went back and lay down again.

I held the puppy while my mother filled the yellow laundry bucket with water. The velvet skin of its head was thick and sealed tight, like a new bud. When the water was deep enough, my mother shut it off and pushed the faucet aside. She looked at me.

"Are you going to do this or do you want me to?" she said. She gazed into my face, waiting. The puppy was warm and dry in my hands; I could smell its sleepy puppy smell.

I looked at my sister. Her mouth was hanging open in a scared little o.

"Put it under?" I whispered. My mother nodded. There was no one else to ask. I walked to the sink and put the puppy's head into the cool water. It jerked and I snatched it back up into the air.

"Don't do that!" my mother said. "You have to hold it there." I put it back under and held it. Its soft body kicked and twitched for a long time in my hands.

My mother stood behind me, watching. "Look how strong," she said. "It's all that good food it got inside the womb."

—

Later, when you have grown, you can live in an apartment at the edge of the city. You can be a vegetarian there, without arguing about it with your mother. You can have one cat and two plants with no purpose but growing. At night, your cat will sleep in the hollow of your arm. In the morning, she will hunt birds. Every week or so she'll catch one, trotting into the bedroom with her victim flapping and screeching in her mouth, and you will leap out of bed with your heart pounding, running to corner her and pry her jaws open before it's too late.

Then the bird, sitting in your hand.

It will be young—you will see its stubby tail feathers, still bound tight in their sheaths; the soft, torn down of its head. You could take it outside and set it free, but you already know it will not fly. Even if you put it on a branch, even if you hide it under a bush, something will come along to kill it—your cat or someone else's; one of those hawks that lives in the park. And you will stand there with the bird in your hand, feeling the faint shiver of its breath, the frantic pulse pumping and pumping under the skin.

ACKNOWLEDGMENTS

This book would never have come to be without the generous help of other people. I am grateful to Rob McQuilkin and Kathryn Belden, my agent and editor, for their willingness to take a chance on me. And I owe a huge debt to my husband, Livy Parsons, who has put up with my need to write, and all the inconvenience and loss of income that entails, for much longer than was probably sensible.

Many dear friends have encouraged and supported me along the way: Deborah Bennett, Eve Bridburg, Daphne Kalotay, Daniela Kukrechtová, Robin Lippert, Carrie Normand, Nina Orville, Jessie Payne, Rishi Reddi, Julie Rold, and Kathy Wolff. A special thanks to the incomparable Judy Layzer, who gave me a vote of confidence when I needed it most, and to the wonderful people who were generous enough to employ an aspiring writer: Linda Sultan, Sara Snyder, Craig Moodie, Brian Nichols, and the good folks at ACCION International.

Susan Meyers and Serine Steakley were there from the

ACKNOWLEDGMENTS

very beginning. Eve Gleichman believed at a time when I was still doubting. Jerry Badanes and Lucy Rosenthal gave me important early encouragement. And Jacquelyn Frohlich has been my faithful companion on this journey for many years. Finally, I am thankful for Nina Payne, without whom I might never have found my way.